Finder

John W. Chambers

FINDER

New York ATHENEUM 1981

Library of Congress Cataloging in Publication Data

Chambers, John W.
    Finder.

    SUMMARY: Jenny and her friends resolve to discover the
secret of the mysterious house hidden in the dunes on Fire
Island after she finds an abandoned dog that seems to
have belonged there.
    [1. Mystery and detective stories. 2. Dogs—
Fiction] I. Title.
PZ7.C3563Fi   [Fic]   80-23928
ISBN 0-689-30803-5

Published simultaneously in Canada by
McClelland & Stewart, Ltd.
Manufactured by Fairfield Graphics, Fairfield, Pennsylvania
Designed by Harry Ford
First Edition

To MARGARET W. CHAMBERS, *who may recognize
a hint of herself in Jenny.*

Contents

1	ARRIVAL	3
2	A FOOT IN THE DOOR	7
3	A DOG NEEDS A NAME	11
4	SUMMER BEGINS	14
5	THE GRAY HOUSE	19
6	FINDER DISAPPEARS	29
7	FOURTH OF JULY	37
8	AN UNLIKELY HERO	46
9	THE TURNING POINT	53
10	JENNY TAKES A CHANCE	66
11	FISH!	74
12	ENCOUNTER	83
13	DETECTIVES AT WORK	96
14	JENNY'S PLAN	108
15	THE SAND CASTLE	113
16	CONFESSION	126
17	PRINCE ABOU	132
18	A MATTER OF TIMING	145
19	PRINCE ABOU RETURNS	151

Finder

North

↑ To Long Island

Great South Bay

PIRATES COVE

ISLAND

FIRE

MARINERS HAVEN

Dune Line

Atlantic Ocean

1. The Gray House
2. Martin House
3. Rollins House
4. Sargeant House

5. Reid House
6. Parks House
7. Pruett House
8. Ketchum House

9. Pritchard House
10. Path to Gray House
11. Docks

1 Arrival

FIRE Island! Jenny Martin stared at the long, flat profile of the island on which she had spent so many summers. It reached as far as the eye could see in either direction: a low-lying, rockless sandbar, guarding the south coast of Long Island and the Great South Bay—which they were now crossing—from the open waters of the North Atlantic. Her parents had been to the island several weekends during the Spring, but this was the first visit of the year for her and her brother Billy. Best of all, it was the start of summer vacation, and three full months stretched before them.

"We're beating the ferry!" Billy called out.

Jenny glanced at the big, cumbersome, white boat

fifty yards ahead, its top deck crowded with day-trippers and weekenders.

"We always beat the ferry," she noted, an edge of sarcasm in her voice. Why did Billy say such stupid things? Of course, he was only ten, two years younger than she was, but that was no excuse. Her friend Betsey's brother was the same age, and he was much more grown-up.

"Hold tight. We're crossing the ferry wake."

Jenny grasped the railing, knees bent to absorb the shock as their boat sliced through the large, foam-capped rollers. Her father was standing behind the center console, his left hand on the wheel and his right on the gearshift. Watching him, Jenny was sorry that she had not asked to drive the boat, but then, remembering the argument at breakfast that morning, she was just as glad. Even thinking about it made her angry all over again. Her father knew that she wanted a dog, so what did he expect her to say when he asked what she wanted for her birthday? He could be thick sometimes. The whole thing was stupid! Lots of people had dogs in New York City. Why did he have to act as if their apartment were some kind of a prison that would make any animal instantly unhappy?

"There's the buoy!"

Jenny looked to where Billy was pointing and saw the buoy that marked the deep-water channel to Mariners Haven.

"Old Man Pritchard is here!" Billy announced.

"I don't see his boat."

"He's got his flag up, see it?"

Jenny shaded her eyes against the sunlight. She saw the flag immediately, grass-green with a white emblem in the center.

"Do you think he's launched yet?" Billy asked, glancing at his father.

Mr. Martin shook his head. "I don't think so. He's been away. I doubt if he's even conditioned his boat."

"Maybe he'll hire me to help him."

"How much are you going to charge?" Jenny asked.

"Same as you charge for baby-sitting; a dollar fifty an hour."

"You should charge two fifty. His boat will need a lot of sanding before it's ready to paint, and that's hard work."

"Maybe I will."

They were very near shore now. Mr. Martin turned the boat into the wind and cut the ignition. Then he slipped into a pair of waders and climbed over the side. While he waded the boat to shore, Jenny helped her mother fold the tarpaulin that covered the luggage and groceries. Then, helped by Billy, they began to pile the boxes, bags, and suitcases on the bow. All was ready for unloading by the time Mr. Martin pulled the boat up to the beach.

Billy, a bag of groceries in either hand, was the first to climb off the boat. Announcing that he would bring the wagon, he hurried up the boardwalk toward the house. He had to pause twice, however, to shift his load, and that gave Jenny, who was carrying a large box, time to catch up. She was just behind him when he turned into the walk that led to the front steps. Suddenly he stopped.

"What's the matter?" Jenny asked impatiently.

"Look."

Jenny looked over his shoulder. Crawling out from under the house was a dog: a soft, brown, cuddly bundle of half-grown puppy with ears cocked expectantly. Jenny stared, not believing her eyes.

"It's a dog," Billy said softly. "It's a dog under our house."

But Jenny didn't hear him. She was already crouched beside the dog, petting it and talking to it. She was still there moments later when her mother arrived at the house.

2 A Foot in the Door

WHERE did that come from?"

Although Mrs. Martin didn't identify the *that*, Jenny had no trouble guessing what she meant and quickly explained that the dog had been under their house. "It likes you, Mommy," she added. The dog was looking up at Mrs. Martin with a puzzled expression, its tail wagging ever so slightly.

"That's hardly the question, Jen," Mrs. Martin replied, her eyes on the dog. Jenny was relieved to see that she was smiling. Finally she turned to Billy. "You'd better get the wagon, Billy. Your father's waiting."

"Do you think we can keep it?" Jenny asked.

"It all depends." Mrs. Martin unlocked the door and picked up the packages that she had set on the deck. She glanced quickly at Jenny. "The dog probably belongs to someone else. We'll have to find out."

"What if it doesn't?"

"We'll just have to wait and see."

With that she turned and stepped into the house, while Jenny hurried down the boardwalk to help Billy and her father. At first the dog seemed to want to follow her, but it soon stopped, glancing hesitantly back toward the house. Jenny purposely ignored it. She was hoping it wouldn't follow her. That way her father wouldn't see it until he came up the walk.

When she reached the bay, she found that Billy and her father had finished unloading, and Mr. Martin was wading the boat back to the permanent mooring, while Billy loaded the wagon. She helped him, and they were ready to start back to the house well before Mr. Martin had finished tying up. Picking up two suitcases that didn't fit on the wagon, Jenny followed Billy up the walk, leaving a final heavy box for Mr. Martin. Halfway to the house they were met by the dog, but they did not stop. Both were only too aware of Mr. Martin wading to the shore behind them. As they approached the house, their mother appeared in the doorway.

"Did your father see the dog?" she asked.

"No."

Mrs. Martin looked toward the bay. "I think I'll walk down and have a word with Daddy."

"About the dog?"

Mrs. Martin nodded.

"Can we go to the beach?" Billy asked.

"Yes, if you promise not to go into the water. Don't stay more than half an hour."

"We won't," Jenny assured her.

Taking off their shoes and socks, she and Billy ran up the boardwalk toward the ocean with the dog bouncing along behind them. Jenny glanced back once, but then they reached the crest of the dune and saw the ocean. The water was wild, the waves breaking in great showers of spray. For some time they stood without moving, their ears deafened by the roar. Then they ran forward, shouting back and forth as they slogged through the loose sand of the upper beach with the dog at their heels.

When they reached the water's edge, they found steep sand cliffs, and they made a game of leaping off them, and then scrambling back just in time to avoid the next wave. It was great fun, and the dog seemed to enjoy the game as much as they did. They were still at it when their mother and father appeared over the rim of the dune. Billy noticed them first and motioned to Jenny. She turned and waved, and ran to meet them, followed by Billy and the dog.

"Who's your friend?" Mr. Martin inquired as they came up to him.

"What friend?" Jenny asked.

"The one with four legs and a tail who's giving me the eye."

Jenny looked down, pushing the sand with her foot. "That's the dog," she mumbled.

"Somehow I knew it wasn't a giraffe," Mr. Martin observed, laughing. "Is he friendly?"

Jenny looked up quickly. "He's *very* friendly, Daddy." She hesitated. "Do you think we can keep him?"

"We'll have to see if he belongs to anyone first. Someone must have brought him here."

"It could be they just left him."

"If it were fall, I'd agree with you, but this is June. People are arriving, not leaving." He squatted down, and the dog stepped over to be petted. He stroked its head, and then scratched it behind the ears. "We'll keep him until we find out if he belongs to anyone."

"What if he doesn't?" Jenny asked.

"If two weeks go by and nobody claims him, we'll have to talk about it again. But don't get up any false hopes," he added quickly. "Chances are he belongs to someone."

"If he doesn't, can we keep him at least for the rest of the summer?"

"We'll cross that bridge when we come to it."

Giving the dog a final pat, he rose to his feet and led the way back toward the house. Billy followed, and then Mrs. Martin, with Jenny and the dog bringing up the rear. Jenny was reasonably satisfied. She had her father's promise of two weeks, and she knew that if the dog were still with them after two weeks, her mother would see to it that he stayed on. As for what would happen at summer's end, that was a long way off.

3 A Dog Needs a Name

AFTER breakfast the next morning, Mr. Martin wrote two identical notices describing the dog, and Jenny and Billy hiked east and then west to post them on the community bulletin boards in Pirates Cove and Mariners Haven. For the next two weeks Jenny worried every time a stranger strolled to their part of the beach, but no one came to claim the dog, nor did anyone telephone about it.

The dog, meanwhile, had made himself very much at home. During the day he stuck close to Jenny and Billy, and at night he slept under Jenny's bed. He had short legs, a long, thin body, and a hunting dog's instincts. Mr. Martin thought that he was roughly one-third dachshund, one-third beagle, and one-third spaniel, but everybody had their own guess about what had gone into the mix. In any case he proved to be little trouble. He was housebroken, and he readily adapted to the Martins' way of life. As Jenny had anticipated, by the time two weeks had passed, they had become so used to the dog that her father did not even mention the deadline.

Naming the dog was not easy, because Jenny wanted the name to be something special. She kept putting it off, until one evening at supper her father observed that he was tired of calling their new pet *dog*.

"Come on, Jen," he urged, "you've had lots of time. Let's have a name for this beast."

Jenny looked down at the dog. He was watching her with his usual head-cocked attention. She thought quickly, reviewing the various names she had considered.

"He looks like a seal waiting for Jen to throw him a fish," Mr. Martin commented, winking at Billy. "Doesn't he remind you of Snoopy?"

"Hey, that's what we should call him!" Billy exclaimed, turning to his sister. "What do you say, Jen? Do you want to call him Snoopy?"

Jenny shook her head. It was a typical Billy suggestion. Everybody was calling his or her dog Snoopy. "Let's call him Finder," she said softly.

"Finder?" Billy stared at her in genuine puzzlement. "Why Finder?"

"Because he found us instead of us finding him."

"Seems like a funny name for a dog."

"I think it's a good name; shows imagination." Mr. Martin glanced at Billy, then back at Jenny. "I like it."

"It's nowhere," Billy scoffed.

"It is not!" Jenny flared back.

"Let's see what the dog thinks." Squatting down, Mr. Martin called the name softly under his breath. The dog looked at him, and sensing the invitation, stepped over to be petted. "I guess that does it," Mr. Martin said. "Finder it will be." He looked at Jenny. "But Jen, remember; no dogs in New York City."

Jenny nodded but said nothing. She recognized the tone and knew there was no point in arguing. Now wasn't the time. Nonetheless, she promised herself that it wasn't going to be as easy as her father thought. She had her dog, and she intended to keep him.

4 Summer Begins

I'M here!"

Jenny jumped to her feet and turned to find Lauren Reid standing behind her, grinning from ear to ear. Lauren was Jenny's best friend on Fire Island, and she had been looking forward eagerly to her arrival.

"When did you get here?" she asked breathlessly.

"Just now. The Rollins came, too, and the Parkses are coming tomorrow."

"How about the Sargeants?"

"They'll be here Saturday. Where's the dog Billy was telling me about?"

14

Jenny called Finder, who emerged from the shrubbery behind the house and trotted over to be petted. Lauren knelt down to examine him. "He's cute," she allowed, as she scratched him behind the ears and rubbed his back. "Where did you get him?"

"He crawled out from under the house the day we got here."

"Where do you think he came from?"

"We don't know." Jenny looked down at her pet, shaking her head. "He's really smart. He even makes Daddy laugh."

"Is he housebroken?"

"Sure."

"Then he must have belonged to someone."

"So what if he did? We put up notices, but nobody's come to claim him."

"They may not have seen the notices."

"The notices are still up. I checked the other day."

Lauren nodded, looking down at Finder thoughtfully. "You know what I'd do," she said. "If he's as smart as you say, he'll know where he came from. You ought to walk down the island with him and see if he recognizes any place."

"What if he does? What do I do then?"

"You find out who lives there."

Jenny stared at Lauren. The idea was so simple it frightened her. "I don't think he came from any house on the beach," she said finally. "I think someone just left him, or maybe he wandered away from someone's boat."

"It won't hurt to find out. If he belongs to someone, it would be better to find out now than later. I'll walk with you."

Jenny reached down to pet Finder. She didn't particularly like the idea, but she couldn't think of any good way to refuse. After all, if Finder had strayed away, it was only fair that she should try to return him. It made her mad though. If Finder had been Lauren's dog, she wondered just how anxious Lauren would have been to walk down the island looking for his owner!

"You know what?" Lauren suggested abruptly. "I think we should take Ron Rollins with us. He really knows the island. If Finder turns up a path, Ron will be able to tell us where it leads."

Jenny nodded. It was a good point. Although he was her age, Ron was Billy's best friend, and the two boys had spent many hours following the deer trails and roaming the marshlands and the sunken forests of the island. In fact, Mr. Ketchum, the naturalist of the community, said that Ron already knew more about the island's biology than even the best informed Park Ranger.

"When do you want to go?" Jenny asked.

"Let's go around one o'clock. I've got to unpack and help Mom clean up the house. Have you seen Ron yet?"

Jenny shook her head.

"He's a monster. He's almost as tall as his father."

Jenny laughed, trying to imagine the new Ron. "He's going to look funny walking around with Billy.

They'll be like Mutt and Jeff."

"They already are. He and Ty had their first fight."

"When?"

"We were all here Memorial Day Weekend. Ron set out a bird net, and Ty put all the dead mice in it that he had caught in the traps his family set. Ron was ready to kill him."

"What did he do to him?"

"Nothing. He couldn't catch him."

They both laughed. Ty was nine years old, and he and his twin sister, Win, could outrun any of the others.

"I'm glad everybody's coming back," Jenny said. "Even the twins."

"Especially the twins. Life would be boring without them."

The two girls were silent after that until Lauren suggested Jenny come to her house. After telling her mother where she was going, Jenny followed Lauren, with Finder trailing behind. On the way Lauren asked what Jenny and Billy had been doing, and Jenny told her that Billy had been going over to the mainland to help Mr. Pritchard condition his boat, while she had been getting a jump on her summer reading and helping her mother plant the garden.

"It's been fun being the only ones here. Besides, I've been getting to know Finder."

"Does he like the water?" Lauren asked.

"He wades in the bay all the time. He even caught an eel the other day. He likes riding in the boat, too."

"Does he go off much?"

Jenny shook her head. "He sticks pretty close. That's why I think maybe he was just left here. If he'd wandered away from some house, it seems to me he'd go back there."

"You're probably right," Lauren agreed. "What's your friend Betsey doing this summer?"

Jenny told her and asked about one of Lauren's friends. Not having seen each other for eight months, they had a lot to talk about, and the time passed rapidly. Jenny had almost forgotten their plan to walk down the island when Lauren observed that it was one o'clock.

"I'll bet Ron and Billy are over at Ron's house. Let's see if they'll come with us."

Leading the way, Lauren hurried off with Jenny and Finder close behind. As Lauren had predicted, Billy and Ron were sitting on Ron's back deck. While Finder and Ron's collie, Rex, were becoming acquainted, Lauren told the boys her idea. They fell in with it immediately, and the four of them started toward the bay with Finder and Rex in the lead. Jenny brought up the rear. She didn't really want to go, but in a way she was just as glad. After all, this would pretty well settle it. She promised herself that tomorrow she would take down the notices describing Finder. They had been up long enough.

5 The Gray House

WHEN they reached the bay, they turned west toward Mariners Haven. On the way they stuck close to the shore. Once Rex started to bark off to their left, but the undergrowth was extremely thick at that point, and even Ron didn't suggest that they try to reach him. A few yards further on they turned into a narrow trail that led inland, following it to a wide, cleared space in the midst of a grove of wild cherries. This was one of their favorite places. Who had cleared it and why was a mystery, but it was cool and shady, and they often used it as a secret meeting place, unknown to adults. While the girls sat down on stumps and talked, Ron and Billy scanned the edges of the clearing, looking for tracks.

Suddenly Ron called to the others, and they quickly joined him. The ground dipped sharply where they were standing, and perched in a hollow in the trunk of a scrub oak was a small owl. It blinked at them placidly with its round, heavy-lidded eyes, its talons tightening and loosening rhythmically in the half-rotted wood. While they were watching, Finder came to investigate, and Jenny picked him up, pointing his head so that he would see the owl. He saw it instantly and squirmed to get loose from Jenny's arms.

"Put him down," Ron suggested. "Let's see what he does."

Jenny put Finder down, and immediately the dog dashed to the foot of the tree, barking furiously. The owl hardly seemed to notice, except that its talons tightened and remained tight. Finder was circling the tree now, whining softly. Suddenly he ran back toward them, jumping onto a broken limb that led toward the owl. Although the angle was steep, Finder inched his way up. When he had almost reached the owl's level, he let out a sharp yip. This was too much for the bird, and it took off, disappearing rapidly among the trees. Bursting with pride, Jenny turned to Ron.

"What do you think of that?" she asked.

"I think your dog's crazy," Ron replied, laughing. "You'd better get him off that tree before he falls off."

After Jenny had lifted Finder down from the tree limb, they returned to the bay. As they came closer to Mariners Haven, Finder seemed to become more and more excited and stuck very close to them. Then suddenly he ran ahead and turned into a narrow trail, barking to catch their attention. When they reached it, they stopped, and Jenny turned to Ron.

"Where does this go?" she asked.

"It goes to a house."

"Who owns it?"

"I don't know. I've seen people there once or twice, but I couldn't tell if they were owners or renters. You can't see the house from the beach. It's down in a hollow."

"Maybe Finder came from there," Lauren suggested, glancing quickly at Jenny.

"It could be," Ron agreed. "He sure seems to know the way."

Jenny watched Finder, and then turned to study the entrance to the trail. She was suddenly afraid. Maybe Finder *had* come from the house in there. She glanced quickly at Lauren, but her friend was watching Finder. It was Billy who broke the uneasy silence.

"Don't you think we ought to talk to them?" he asked. "Maybe Finder belongs to them."

Jenny knew that they were leaving the decision to her. She knew, too, that she didn't have a choice. To turn back now would only delay the inevitable. She couldn't keep Finder away all summer. Besides, someone was sure to say something, and once her parents heard the story, they would insist that the people be contacted.

"I guess we'd better walk up to the house," she said quietly.

Ron led the way, with Finder and Rex running on

ahead. For the first twenty-five yards, the trail climbed steadily. Then it topped a ridge and turned slightly east. Ahead of them they saw the house. It was small, and as Ron had said, it was well hidden in a little clearing surrounded by foliage. The dogs had already reached it and were circling the yard, sniffing and exploring. Finder seemed particularly excited. He was standing near the front door, whining softly, as they came up to him, and Jenny stepped over to pet him, talking soothingly in a low voice. Although there was apparently no one in the house, people had evidently been staying there recently. They could tell that from the number of footprints in the sand. Billy pointed to the tanks of bottled gas near the back door.

"I wonder how they get their gas?" he asked.

"They probably haul it up from the bay," Lauren guessed.

"They do." Ron pointed to a long, shallow trench in the sand. Stepping past Billy, he tried to lift each tank in turn. "Feels like they're full."

"They must be coming back then."

"Probably." Ron turned, watching Jenny and Finder. "You know, if your dog comes from here, it's funny he hasn't tried to come back before. It's not that far."

"Maybe his owner was trying to get rid of him," Lauren suggested.

"Why would he do that?"

"How should I know? People do funny things."

Ron laughed. "Dogs do, too. Look at Rex. What the dickens does he think he's doing?"

Next to the kitchen door there was a platform on

which firewood was piled. Rex was on his side, trying to squeeze under it. After watching him briefly, Ron lay down next to him, his head flat to the ground. Slowly he inched forward, apparently reaching for something. Grasping it, he wiggled back and got to his feet.

"What is it?" Jenny asked.

"Nothing. Just some rolled up newspaper. Hey, that's funny. Look at this."

Jenny looked, and she, too, was puzzled. "That's a funny kind of writing. Do you think it could be Chinese?"

Ron shook his head. "I don't think so. I've seen Chinese writing, and it didn't look like this. This is more like a script."

He handed it to Jenny, who held it in front of her, looking at it carefully. "I know what we'll do," she said finally. "We'll show it to Mr. Pritchard. Maybe he can tell us what language it is."

"How would he know?"

"He's been to a lot of foreign places. If anybody can tell us, he can."

"Hey, look here," Lauren called abruptly. She had climbed the back steps and was holding a note, which had been slipped under the door. "It looks like it's written in the same language."

Jenny took it and looked at it. "I think it is," she agreed.

She hesitated, surveying the clearing a final time. Then, folding the newspaper and the note and putting them in her pocket, she called Finder and led the way down to the bay. At first Finder was reluctant to leave the house, but by the time they neared the shore, he was running along beside Jenny and no longer whining. At the entrance to the path they stopped to look around and quickly discovered a mashed-down strip of foliage where a boat had apparently been dragged out of the water.

"Probably a dory," was Ron's conclusion as he surveyed the spot. "They must anchor a bigger boat out further."

"We should watch for it," Billy suggested.

"Let's go see Mr. Pritchard."

With Jenny leading, they hurried back to Mid Station. Before they could reach Mr. Pritchard's house, however, Mr. Pruett, the old retired actor who owned the bay house on Mr. Pritchard's walk, spotted them and asked where they had been. When they told him about the gray house and the newspaper in a foreign language, he put on his reading glasses to look at it.

"I know what it is," he said finally, "but that doesn't signify that I know what it means."

"What is it?" Jenny asked.

"It's a sheet of newspaper . . ." Mr. Pruett paused, watching his audience over the tops of his glasses and purposely stretching the suspense, ". . . in Arabic."

"Arabic!" they exclaimed.

"Arabic," Mr. Pruett affirmed. *"The barge she sat in, like a burnished throne, burned on the water . . ."* He paused again, regarding them owlishly. "Shakespeare."

"Does that mean that it's an Arabian newspaper?" Jenny asked.

Mr. Pruett shook his head. "Not necessarily. It could have come from any of the countries that speak Arabic: Saudi Arabia, Algeria, Tunisia, Morocco; there are quite a number of them. If I were you, I'd have a talk with our old friend Pritchard. He's spent a lot of time in that part of the world."

"We were on our way to his house," Jenny told him. "Is he home?"

Mr. Pruett glanced up the walk. "I imagine so, unless he be *contending with the fretful elements* out on the bay."

Jenny looked up quickly. "Shakespeare?"

"Lear, Act Three, Scene One."

Leaving Mr. Pruett, they hurried up the walk to the small shack on the dune end of Bachelors Walk where Mr. Pritchard lived. They found him outside his house, touching up the lettering on the sign that carried his name. He finished the curl on the "d" before he put down his brush and asked what they wanted.

"We want to ask you something," Jenny replied, handing the sheet of newspaper to him. "Can you tell us what country this comes from?"

"Can't tell you anything without my glasses. The old eyes aren't what they used to be. Come on in."

Opening the door, he waited while the children filed past him. When the dogs started to follow, he shooed them away and stepped in himself.

Mr. Pritchard's shack was crude but comfortable. It

consisted of three rooms: a bedroom, a living room, and a kitchen. As they stepped into the living room, they found the central table spread with newspaper and a big pot of crabs next to it. They had already been boiled and were bright red in color.

"Anybody want to start cleaning crabs while we're talking?" Mr. Pritchard called from the kitchen.

"I will," Billy called back, and he and Ron sat down on either side of the table and began to strip the claws and shells, pulling out the deadman and the gills to get at the sweet, white meat locked in the long capsules of cartilage. Jenny did not watch. She disliked crabs to begin with, and she particularly disliked the job of cleaning them. She looked up as Mr. Pritchard stepped into the room, wearing his glasses, the sheet of news-paper in his hand.

"Where did you find this?" he asked.

"We found it outside a house on the east end of Mari-ners Haven," Jenny replied.

"This is an Egyptian newspaper. Judging from the news, I'd guess it's no more than a month old."

"Can you read it?" Lauren asked.

Mr. Pritchard laughed. "Bless your heart, I lived there long enough I should be able to read it. I wonder how an Egyptian newspaper got to Mariners Haven?"

"That's what we were wondering." Jenny glanced at Lauren and turned to Mr. Pritchard. "Finder seems to know the house, too. He led us to it.

"That little dog of yours? I guess you did a pretty good job of naming him."

"Do you think he could have come from Egypt?"

"Him?" Mr. Pritchard looked through the window to where the dogs were lying on the porch and smiled broadly. "Whatever else they have in Egypt for export, I don't think you're going to find dogs one of the hotter items. That dog's purebred American mutt if I ever saw one."

Getting slowly to his feet, he walked to the bedroom door and hung the newspaper on a nail.

"Mind if I keep this?" he asked, glancing at Jenny.

She shook her head. "We found something else." Taking the note out of her pocket, she handed it to him. "It was partway under the back door."

Mr. Pritchard took the note and studied it. Then he put it in his pocket.

"What does it say?" Ron asked.

Mr. Pritchard looked at him. "I shouldn't tell you," he said finally, "but I think I will. One condition: don't mention it to anybody. Understand?"

They all nodded.

"The note reads: *No police report.*"

Jenny was the first to recover from her surprise. "What do you think it means?" she asked.

"No way to know, but I'll tell you what you might do. Drop by that house again some time next week and see if you can find out who's living there. Don't make a big point of it, but see what you can discover. It might be interesting, and who's going to get mad at a bunch of kids. But be careful," he added. "You just happen to be walking through. If they tell you to clear out, you clear out."

He looked around the circle, and they looked back at him solemnly.

"Okay?"

Jenny looked at the others, then nodded. "Okay."

6 Finder Disappears

A FTER they left Mr. Pritchard's house, Jenny and the others walked up toward the ocean. When they reached the dune line, they stopped to look over the beach.

"Hey, there's Ty and Win!"

Jenny looked to where Ron was pointing. She saw Win immediately, but it was several seconds before she saw Ty. Then he appeared from behind a tremendous pile of sand, a shovel over his shoulder.

"It looks like they've dug up half the beach. Let's see what they're up to."

With Ron leading the way, they hurried to the spot where the twins were working. As he came up to

them, Ron asked what they were doing. He had to re-
peat the question, and even then Ty barely glanced at
him.

"What do you think we're doing? We're digging a
hole."

"Why?"

"Cause we want to."

Ty was pushing the sand back from the edge now.
Win stood next to him, looking down into the hole.

"Think it's deep enough?"

"Almost."

"Deep enough for what?" Ron asked again.

"Deep enough for what we want."

"What do you want?"

"Wouldn't you like to know?"

Ignoring Ron, Ty plunged the shovel into the hole,
marking the depth by grasping the handle at ground
level. Then he pulled it out, and he and Win stared at
it critically. Jenny guessed that the hole was over five
feet deep.

"I think it ought to be a foot deeper," Win said
finally.

Ron did not particularly like the twins in the first
place, and he hated being ignored. Without bothering
to ask more questions, he shoved Ty out of the way and
stepped to the edge of the hole to look in. That was a
mistake. Quick as a cat, Ty jumped behind him and
pushed. For a fraction of a second Ron teetered on the
edge, his arms flailing the air. Then he slipped in,
while Ty let out a triumphant whoop of laughter.

"You want to know what it is?" he crowed. "It's a

garbage pit, and you're the garbage in it!"

Without waiting to see more, Ty picked up the shovel, and he and Win took off for their house at top speed. They were none too soon. Ron caught Billy's hand and was out of the hole and after the twins in an instant. For a few seconds the race was close, but the twins were skinny and had long legs, and before Ron had reached the crest of the dune line, the two were on their doorstep. Ty turned to thumb his nose at Ron, who shook a fist at him, shouting that he would get him, but Ty only laughed and ducked inside.

After the twins had disappeared, Ron led the way to his house. There was a big deck on the north side, and here they settled to talk. At first they talked about the twins. Actually Jenny thought Ron deserved the trick they had played on him. He could be a bully at times, and it served him right if Ty was smart enough to fool him. Ron always said that he didn't trust the twins, but it was Jenny's experience that they never lied. Of course, they rarely volunteered the truth if it was not to their advantage, but that was not really a fault. She didn't either.

Anyway she had more important things to think about. Now that it appeared that Finder had come from the gray house, she wanted to learn more about the people who lived there, but she was a little frightened, too. She didn't want to lose Finder, and besides, the reference to the police made it sound just a little scary.

"When do you want to go back to the gray house?" Lauren asked abruptly, and Jenny turned to find that the others were watching her. She thought for a moment, turning it over in her mind, and made her decision.

"Let's go on Saturday."

"Can't. Saturday's the clambake."

Lauren was right. Fourth of July weekend was coming up, and Saturday night would be the clambake. Besides, it would serve no purpose to go back to the gray house until the occupants had returned.

"Let's wait until Monday," Jenny said finally, and the others agreed. Then they talked about one thing and another until Jenny suddenly noticed that Finder was nowhere in sight.

"When was the last time you saw Finder?" she asked Billy.

"Up on the beach. He and Rex were down near the entrance to Bachelors Walk."

"Has anyone seen him since then?"

They all shook their heads.

"He and Rex probably went hunting," Ron suggested.

"Finder doesn't usually go off," Jenny noted. She looked down at the deck. Then she turned again to Ron. "Do you think he could have gone back to the gray house in Mariners Haven?"

"Why would he have gone there? He hasn't tried to go before, has he?"

"We haven't walked there before today."

"So?"

"So maybe he went back."

Ron shook his head. "I'll bet you'll find him down

at the bay. Heck, Rex goes off all the time."

"Maybe, but I want to be sure."

Getting to her feet, Jenny turned to Lauren. "I'm going to walk down to the bay to look for him. Want to come?"

Lauren nodded, and the two girls quickly left the deck. After checking at the Martin house, they hurried down to the bay. There was no sign of Finder. Jenny walked out to the end of the dock, looking left and right along the shore. She was becoming increasingly worried. On the one hand it seemed silly. After all, Finder had been with them for almost a month and had shown no desire to leave. And yet, if the gray house had been his home, now that he had found it again, mightn't he want to return to it?

"What do we do now?" Lauren asked as Jenny walked back to shore.

"Let's walk up toward the gray house."

"Do you think he went back there?"

"He might have."

Turning toward Mariners Haven, Jenny started down the shore. Seconds later she came to an abrupt halt.

"Look there!" she exclaimed, pointing up ahead. "See that boat? I think it's anchored off the gray house."

Lauren looked to where Jenny was pointing, squinting against the glare. "I think you're right," she agreed.

The two girls stood motionless, studying the boat. It was a long, trim cabin cruiser with an inboard engine. Apparently no one was aboard.

"I don't think we'd better go up there," Lauren whispered nervously.

"Why not?"

"We might meet someone."

"So what if we do? We've got a perfect right to walk along the bayshore. Let's at least go to the path."

"All right. But no further."

Again Jenny led the way, and Lauren followed. When they reached the path, they found a dory pulled well up on shore. Jenny stepped over to examine it.

"It looks new."

She turned toward the path. She was tempted to walk up it, but as she started, her eye was caught by a NO TRESPASSING sign nailed to a nearby tree.

"That wasn't there this morning, was it?" she asked, glancing at Lauren.

"I don't think so. Does it say who owns the property?"

"No. It just says trespassers will be prosecuted by the owner. Does that mean arrested?"

"I guess so."

Jenny studied the sign. Then she glanced up the path. Finally she turned away reluctantly. "I guess we'd better not go up there."

"I don't think we should either," Lauren agreed hastily. "It doesn't look as if they want to have visitors."

On the way back they barely spoke. Finally Jenny asked Lauren if she thought Finder had gone back to the gray house.

"I think he went hunting," Lauren replied. "Why would he have gone back to the gray house? He must not have had a very good home, or they wouldn't have left him in the first place. *You* wouldn't leave a dog."

"Maybe they didn't mean to leave him."

"But they did, and you and I wouldn't."

Jenny nodded. She hoped Lauren was right. Just before they reached Mid Station, they met Ron and Billy walking toward them.

"Did you find him?" Billy asked as soon as he saw them.

"No. Has Rex come back?"

"He's at the house," Ron replied. "He came back about five minutes after you left. Hey," he added, pointing behind them, "isn't that boat anchored off the path to the gray house?"

"It is, and there's a dory pulled up on shore. And you know what else? They've put up a 'no trespassing' sign."

"A 'no trespassing' sign?"

"Yes. It's nailed to the tree at the foot of the path."

"No kidding!" Ron glanced at Billy and whistled softly. "You know, that's really strange. I never heard of anyone putting up a 'no trespassing' sign on the beach. People just don't do it." He stared at the boat anchored out in the bay. Then he turned to the others. "What do you think? Should we walk up by the house the way Mr. Pritchard told us?"

"We'd better not. Let's wait and see if Finder comes back."

"Jenny's right," Lauren agreed quickly. "Besides, when Mr. Pritchard told us, they hadn't nailed up that 'no trespassing' sign."

"Think we should talk to him again?"

"Let's just wait."

Taking a last glance at the boat, Jenny turned and led the way back to Mid Station.

7 Fourth of July

F INDER did not appear that night, nor did he turn up the next day. Jenny called him frequently, and twice she walked toward the gray house, pausing at the bay end of the path and calling his name, but there was no sign of him. Finally on Friday night he returned.

The Martins had been eating a late supper, and they were just about to get up from the table, when there was a scratching at the door. Jenny was out of her seat immediately and across the room to open the door. It was Finder. Jenny dropped to her knees, pulling him tight against her. Finder whimpered softly and wiggled and squirmed in his efforts to lick her face and neck. Then suddenly he let out a yelp. Jenny put him down quickly, afraid that she had somehow hurt him.

"What's the matter?" Billy asked.

"I don't know. I was petting him, and suddenly . . ." She let the thought trail off as she was struck by something else. "Look! He's got a piece of rope around his neck. Somebody must have tied him up."

Billy knelt to look, and he saw something that had escaped Jenny's scrutiny. "Dad," he called, "come look. He's got a bruise on his back leg. It must hurt him, too, because he doesn't like me to touch it."

Mr. Martin walked over, and squatting down, probed delicately with his fingers at the place Billy indicated.

"He does have a bruise. Billy, will you get the ST?"

"Are you going to put ST on a dog?" Billy asked.

Mr. Martin looked up, grinning. "Why not? It's a mild disinfectant. I don't know why it won't work as well for a dog as it would for you and me."

"Do you think it's infected?" Jenny asked.

"No. I just want to make sure it doesn't become infected."

"Are you going to put a bandage on it?"

"Not worth it. Finder would have it off in no time. Thanks, Billy."

Taking the bottle of ST and a cotton pad, Mr. Martin soaked the cotton and placed it against the bruise on Finder's leg. At first Finder tried to move away, but then he stood and allowed Mr. Martin to dab gently at the spot.

"How do you think it happened?" Jenny asked.

"I would guess he was kicked."

Jenny glanced at Billy. "I'll bet it happened at the gray house."

"What gray house?" her father asked quickly, looking up at her.

"The gray house in Mariners Haven." Jenny hesitated. *Would her father try to take Finder back if she told him? But how could he? If they had kicked Finder and tied him up, it would be cruel to take him back there.* Her mind made up, she told about finding the gray house and about her last trip there with Lauren when they had seen the freshly tacked-up 'No Trespassing' sign. Mr. and Mrs. Martin were astonished, and they were silent for some time before Mr. Martin asked if Jenny and the others were intending to return to the gray house.

"Mr. Pritchard said we should," Billy replied. "He said if we went up there in a bunch, no one could really object, and we might learn something."

Mrs. Martin was indignant. "He's got his nerve sending other peoples' children off to snoop!"

"It wouldn't be snooping, Mom," Billy argued. "We'd just be looking while we passed through."

"What do you think about that, Stu?" Mrs. Martin asked, ignoring Billy.

Mr. Martin looked at her, and then turned to Jenny. "If I were you kids, I'd give that house a wide berth. If people want privacy, that's their right, and a 'no trespassing' sign means what it says. Other people have no business ignoring it."

"What if Finder goes back there again?" Jenny asked.

"If he was tied up and kicked, I doubt that he will. On the other hand, if that's where he came from, and the tying and kicking happened somewhere else, then he probably will go back sooner or later. You wouldn't want to keep him from returning to his rightful owner, would you?"

"What do you think about the Egyptian newspaper and the note?" Billy asked.

"The newspaper probably indicates that someone who's Egyptian is renting the house or was a guest there. About the note I'd just as soon not speculate. The fact remains, it's none of your business, and I don't want you going back there."

"What if we meet the people on the beach?" Jenny asked.

"If you do, you do. Just don't make nuisances of yourselves."

Soon after, Jenny went to bed. Finder slept in her room, and the following day he stuck very close to her. It was a busy day, because the Fourth of July clambake was scheduled for the evening. Billy went out after breakfast to help with the clamming, while Jenny went to Lauren's house to shuck corn. Lauren jumped to her feet the moment she saw Finder.

"When did Finder come back?" she asked excitedly.

"Last night," Jenny replied.

After greeting Finder enthusiastically, Lauren sat down to resume her job, and Jenny sat down beside her and began to help while she told the story. After she had finished, they speculated about where Finder had been and what had happened to him.

"Did you notice that the boat's gone?" Lauren asked, breaking a brief silence.

Jenny didn't have to ask which boat. She knew that Lauren meant the boat that had been anchored off the path to the gray house.

"It left last night," Lauren added. "I saw them rowing out to it when I went down to tie up our dory."

"How many people were there?"

"I couldn't tell."

"I mean, were there a lot, or just one or two?"

"There were several. Then one man rowed the dory back to shore."

"They didn't all go then?"

Lauren shook her head. "I guess not." She paused, her glance resting on Finder. "Do you think Finder was at the gray house?"

"Where else could he have gone?"

"He could have gone anywhere. Maybe he went to some house, and the people wanted to keep him and tied him up."

"Why would they have kicked him?"

"Maybe they didn't kick him." Lauren dropped a shucked ear of corn into the bucket and picked up another. "Maybe somebody else kicked him."

Jenny looked at her friend in exasperation. Sometimes it seemed as if Lauren liked to argue just for the sake of arguing. Deciding to ignore her, Jenny concentrated on the corn-shucking. When they had finished, Lauren put the basket on the front porch, and she and Jenny walked down to the dock. Mr. Pruett and Mr. Ketchum were wading in to shore, and Jenny called to them, asking how many clams they had found.

"Enough for you two," Mr. Pruett assured her. "I'd say almost half a bushel, wouldn't you, William?"

"Somewhere near that," Mr. Ketchum agreed, pulling himself up on the dock. "Is that your new dog, Jenny?"

"That's Finder."

Mr. Ketchum studied him thoughtfully. Pulling a pipe from his pocket, he filled it with tobacco, packing it down with his little finger.

"Seems to me I saw a dog just about like him the other day. Only it was tied up."

"Where?" Jenny asked quickly.

"Up to Mariners Haven. It didn't look too happy." He glanced quickly at Jenny. "Could it have been your dog?"

Jenny nodded. "I think it was. He came home last night with a piece of broken rope around his neck. It looked as if he had chewed through it."

"I wouldn't be surprised. Seems like he was chewing on it when I saw him."

"At which house did you see him?" Jenny asked.

Mr. Ketchum smoked for a moment in silence, puffing hard on his pipe to get it burning properly. He had a small, gray mustache, and when he was smoking, the smoke and the mustache seemed to merge, so that his mustache appeared to be flying off his face. It always tickled Jenny, and even now she could not suppress a half-smothered giggle. Mr. Pruett glanced at her but said nothing.

"Well, that was yesterday morning, and I was walking up that way because I wanted to see how many deer were using the freshwater swamp just this side of Mariners Haven. You know the one I mean?"

The girls nodded.

"This time of year there's plenty of graze, but the water begins to get scarce. Generally the deer bunch up near a water hole where they can have plenty to eat and drink. Besides, there are a lot of ferns and moss that grow there, and I like to see how many kinds I can identify." He glanced at them quickly. "Have I ever taken you two on a nature walk into one of the swamps on the island?"

Jenny shook her head.

"I'll do it one of these days. I think you'd enjoy the experience." He paused again, watching Finder, who was hunting in the shallow water. "Anyway, it was on the way back from the swamp that I noticed your dog there. He was tied to one of the locust posts under that gray house on the east end of the Haven."

Jenny glanced quickly at Lauren. "Do you know who owns it?" she asked Mr. Ketchum.

"Man from the city. He doesn't come out much though. Usually rents the place."

"Does he have it rented now?"

"I expect so. There were some foreign-looking people around the place."

Jenny was about to ask another question, but Mr. Ketchum motioned to Mr. Pruett, and the two of them picked up their clam basket and started up the boardwalk. After they had gone, Jenny and Lauren decided to go back to their houses for lunch.

When Jenny returned to the house, she found the family already eating. She thought of telling them what Mr. Ketchum had told her, but decided against it. She could tell Billy later.

Near the end of the afternoon, preparations for the clambake went into high gear. While the men of the community dug a pair of shallow pits, the women and children scavenged for wood. By the time the supply was deemed sufficient, a fire was roaring in each of the pits. Then everyone turned to filling two brand new garbage cans with layers of food, beginning with clams and ending with corn and apple slices. An hour later the cans were placed on pipes over the fires, and all watched in anticipation, listening to the gurglings and assorted cooking noises from inside the metal containers.

The supper was superb. The chicken and vegetables were done to perfection, and after they were eaten, there were the clams, which had been simmering for an hour in their own juices. They were tender and tasty, and the rich broth left at the bottom of the cans was the perfect ending to the meal. Midway through, Billy challenged Ron to a competition to see who could eat the most clams, and Lauren and Skip Sargeant, who was eight, and Jenny urged them on. When Ron finally gave up, he had eaten thirty-six, and Billy was still going. Immediately Billy was crowned the champion clam eater, although Ty Parks was heard to mutter that he could have eaten fifty without half trying.

By this time it was dark, and Mr. Sargeant announced a surprise. Hammering on one of the cans to attract attention, he shouted that if everyone would walk down to the bay, he had a small fireworks display set up. Minutes later the first rocket, a noisemaker, arched into the air, followed by a long series of rockets of various types, until in a grand finale, Mr. Sargeant sent up three together, while the children lit sparklers and whirled them over their heads. Then the penny crackers started going off on all sides, making it sound as if an infantry battle were in progress. It was a grand party, made even more fun by the fireworks displays on the mainland, which could be seen in the distance. When it was over, the only regret was that Fourth of July came just once a year. But it wasn't a very big regret. Everyone was much too tired and satisfied for that.

8 An Unlikely Hero

THE week after Fourth of July weekend, which was also the week of Billy's birthday, seemed to go by in a tremendous rush. Now that the surf was warming up, everyone spent most of their time on the beach. Although swimming was the major activity, Billy and Jenny also practiced surf casting. With Billy's birthday only a few days off, both he and Jenny suspected that he would be getting a surf rod, especially since there was only one rod for the two of them to share.

The gray house was never far from Jenny's thoughts during this time, and she kept a close watch on the bay, hoping to see the cabin cruiser again, but the boat did not return. Twice during the week Finder went off for long periods of time, not coming back until late in the evening, and both times Jenny was extremely worried. She assumed that he was skulking in the vicinity of the gray house, and she was tempted to go there. Although she was relieved when he returned safely, it only served to remind her that her ownership of Finder was still in doubt.

The day of Billy's birthday proved memorable in more ways than one. Billy had been persuaded to go to the mainland to help Ron and his father repair the roof of their house. When he returned early in the afternoon, the party began. There was ice cream and cake, the opening of presents (including the expected casting rod), and then to cap it off, a treasure hunt. The children crisscrossed the island three times, following a series of clues, before Ron found the twelfth and final clue in the valley behind the dune line on the oceanward side of Bachelors Walk. It instructed him to step off six paces east, four south, two west, and dig. Ron paced it and began to dig at the spot indicated, but he found nothing. Puzzled, he turned to the others, but they were baffled, too. Finally, Win Parks suggested that perhaps Ron's paces had been too short, since he was a boy, and a man had written the instructions. This appeared to make sense, and Ron paced it again, taking longer steps. Then he and Billy began to dig. Meanwhile Finder and Rex were digging in the original hole. Suddenly Ty, who was watching the dogs, let out a yell and pushed Finder and Rex out of the way. Seconds later he rose to his feet with a small, metal box clasped firmly in his hands.

"The dogs found it!" he shouted. "The dogs found the treasure!"

"How about that!" exclaimed Mr. Martin, who with Mr. Sargeant and Mr. Rollins was watching, and the three of them burst out laughing. Jenny picked up Finder and hugged him tightly.

"What are you going to give Finder and Rex as a reward?" she asked Billy.

"I'll give each of them a bone. Come on! Let's go back to our place, and I'll divide up the treasure."

At the house Billy quickly divided the coins in the treasure box, and the children gradually drifted off, until only Lauren, Jenny, and Billy remained. When Billy picked up a book that Ron had given him and started to read, Jenny and Lauren strolled down to the bay. Walking out on the dock, they looked out over the water.

"Look, Jen, the boat's back!" Lauren announced excitedly.

Jenny looked up toward Mariners Haven. Now that they knew what to look for, it was easy to recognize the sleek silhouette of the cabin cruiser.

"Have you and Billy gone back to the gray house since the time we all went up there?" Lauren asked.

"No. Dad told us not to. Why?"

"I walked up to Mariners Haven yesterday afternoon, and I saw a boy and two men on the beach. I think they might have come from the gray house."

"How old was the boy?"

"About ten or eleven. I couldn't see them very well.

They were back near the dunes."

"What did the men look like?"

"They were both dark with a lot of hair on their arms, and one of them was almost bald. They were kind of foreign looking, and they seemed tough."

"Did the boy talk to them at all?"

"Not while I was there. He was playing in the sand, and they were watching. It was kind of creepy."

Jenny nodded, her eyes on the cabin cruiser. "Maybe we'll walk up there later," she said softly. "Dad didn't say anything about not walking on the beach."

"Are you going to take Finder with you?"

Jenny glanced at Finder, who was as usual wading in the bay, ears cocked attentively. "I don't know. I'll have to think about it. Let's go back to your house and do some sewing."

Leaving Finder wading in the shallows, the two girls walked back to the Reid house. It was almost an hour later when Jenny looked up from her sewing, aware suddenly that a dog was barking in the distance. She put down the blouse she was working on and walked to the door. The barking was loud and insistent, and it appeared to be coming from the direction of the bay.

"Do you think it's Finder?" Lauren asked.

"It sounds like him. Let's go down and have a look. He seems awfully excited."

Putting down their sewing, the two girls walked quickly down to the bay. When they reached the shore, they saw Finder immediately. He was standing in the water near the end of the dock, barking furiously. Wading out to him, Jenny put a hand on his shoulder, asking softly what it was all about. It was only then that she looked in the direction he was facing, and her eyes dilated with shock. Floating far out on the water was the Sargeants' dory, and in it was four year old Paula! Evidently she had untied the boat and gotten into it as she loved to do when her father was clamming, only this time there was a stiff offshore breeze. Before she knew it, she had drifted into water too deep for her, and now she was trapped with the boat floating ever further from shore.

Jenny wasted no time. Calling to Lauren to tell their fathers, she herself ran to the Sargeant house to tell Mr. Sargeant. He raced down to the bay and splashed through the shallow water without stopping. He was soon up to his waist, pushing ahead as fast as he could in pursuit of the dory floating low in the water fifty yards ahead of him.

Lauren meanwhile had told the others, and the Reids and the Martins arrived at the dock almost simultaneously. Realizing that the dory was floating too fast for Mr. Sargeant to catch up to it, Mr. Martin untied his boat. Telling Mrs. Sargeant and Skip to step aboard, he waded out quickly to a depth at which he could start the outboard motor. Then he climbed over the side, started the engine, and threw it into gear, heading out toward the dory. Mr. Sargeant heard the boat coming and turned with obvious relief.

Speeding past him, Mr. Martin did not pause. He wanted to get to the dory as fast as possible. Only when he was a stone's throw away did he slow the boat to a crawl, so that there would be no wake to upset the

smaller boat. Then Skip jumped overboard and swam
to the dory, while Mrs. Sargeant cautioned Paula not
to move. Paula had been crying earlier, but as the boat
floated further and further from shore, her fear had
grown beyond tears, and as Skip commented later, she
looked scared to death.

She watched now in tight-lipped silence as Skip
swam the dory over to the larger boat. Passing the bow
rope to Mr. Martin, he climbed aboard, while Mr.
Martin pulled the dory alongside. Finally Mrs. Sargeant reached down and lifted Paula over the side.
Only then did the tears come. While Mrs. Sargeant
consoled her daughter as best she could, Mr. Martin
secured the dory rope to the stern cleat and started for
shore. He cruised in slowly, stopping to pick up Mr.
Sargeant on the way. It was a tired but relieved family
that stepped off the boat at the Martins' dock. Paula's
crying had abated to a heavy sobbing, and she cuddled
close to her mother for comfort.

When they reached the house, Mrs. Sargeant stepped
inside to put Paula to bed. The others sat outside on
the deck in the twilight, talking over what had happened. Jenny was asked to tell her story again, and
they all speculated on how Paula had managed to get
herself in such a fix. It was Mr. Sargeant who called
attention to Finder.

"There's the one we have to thank," he observed,
pointing to Finder. "If Finder's barking hadn't at-
tracted Jenny's attention, there's no telling what might
have happened. Paula could have panicked at any time
and fallen overboard." He shook his head, his face

grim. "We owe Finder a lot."

"I guess he's kind of a hero," Jenny said softly.

Mr. Sargeant agreed. "You're darned right he is!"

As for Finder, he looked at them contentedly, basking in their appreciation. After all, how many dogs find a treasure and become a hero all in the same day?

9 The Turning Point

WHEN Jenny and Billy looked back on that summer, they both agreed that the Saturday of the week following Billy's birthday had been the turning point. On that day Jenny's suspicions about the inhabitants of the gray house had been transformed into a certainty that there was something wrong.

Saturdays, once the season is fully underway, bring an atmosphere all their own to Fire Island. Although many people come over on Friday night, the bulk of the weekend visitors arrive Saturday morning, and the beach gets more and more crowded as the hours pass. Jenny was always intrigued by this weekend transformation, and she loved to walk to Pirates Cove on a

Saturday morning. On this particular day she went to Lauren's house early. Her mother had asked her to return a quart of milk that the Martins had borrowed, and besides she was hoping to persuade Lauren to walk with her. After giving Mrs. Reid the quart of milk, she asked Lauren if she wanted to take a walk.

"Where to?" Lauren asked.

"Where do you think? Pirates Cove."

"Why not walk to Mariners Haven?"

"Why?"

"We might see something. Remember what I told you about seeing the people from the gray house on the beach?"

Jenny remembered very well. She had been tempted to walk to Mariners Haven the day after Lauren had told her, but at the last minute she had decided not to.

"How do you know the people you saw were from the gray house?"

"I don't, but that's the only house near where they were. Besides, they were foreign looking."

"Let's talk to Mr. Pritchard before we go."

"Why?" Lauren asked.

"Do you know how an Egyptian looks? He can tell us."

As they were about to leave, Lauren's mother called from the kitchen to ask where they were going. Lauren replied that they were going to Mariners Haven.

"Why don't you look up that girl you met last summer, the one on End Walk?" Mrs. Reid suggested.

"Maybe we will."

Closing the door behind them, the girls ran quickly to Mr. Pritchard's house. Seeing no sign of him, they knocked on the door.

"Who is it?" a voice called from inside.

"It's Jenny Martin and Lauren Reid. We want to ask you a question."

"Come on in."

Jenny shoved open the door, and she and Lauren slipped into the house. Mr. Pritchard was sitting at the table, reading a newspaper. When they had settled on the sofa across from him, he asked what was on their minds.

"What do Egyptians look like?"

"What do they look like?" Mr. Pritchard repeated, studying Jenny thoughtfully. "You two must be thinking about that gray house again."

He watched them, his fingers tapping lightly on the table. Jenny noticed that the Egyptian newspaper was still tacked to the wall.

"What are you intending to do?" he asked finally.

"We were just going to walk up the beach and see if we saw them."

"What'll you do if you see them?"

Jenny and Lauren exchanged a quick look, and it was Lauren who answered the question. "We won't do anything. We'll just look at them."

"From what you told me before, they may not like that."

Getting slowly to his feet, Mr. Pritchard walked over to the window and looked out.

"Your mother spoke to me the other day, Jenny. She said she didn't like the sound of this gray house business. She wants you and the other kids to stay away from there."

"We wouldn't be going near the gray house. We'd just be walking on the beach."

"That's begging the issue."

"I don't think it is."

"All right. Walk up there if you want to, but mind your own beeswax!"

"Will you answer our question?"

"What question?"

"About how Egyptians look . . ."

Mr. Pritchard shook his head, and this time he smiled. "You never give up, do you? Well, they probably won't be speaking English, and if they do, it will be with British accents. It's possible, too, that they may be darker-skinned, although with the suntans people develop out here, I wouldn't count on that." He paused, looking at a spot above their heads. "You know what I'd do if I were you? I'd take that dog with you. If they're out there, he'll most likely recognize them."

"What if they try to take him back?"

"That's the risk you run. After all, they have to catch him first. Besides, if he's their dog, he's their dog."

"Mr. Pritchard's right, Jen," Lauren agreed.

Jenny kept her eyes on the floor. On the one side was her curiosity and her desire to learn more, but balancing it was her fear of losing Finder. After all, it wasn't Lauren's dog that they were using for bait!

"Finder won't go back to them," Lauren said firmly.

"Not after what they did to him before."

"I thought you said that happened somewhere else," Jenny reminded her.

"Why would Finder have gone anywhere else?" Lauren glanced at Mr. Pritchard, but he was reading his paper again. "Come on, Jen. Let's go get Finder."

Climbing reluctantly to her feet, Jenny followed Lauren to the door. As they were going out, Mr. Pritchard told them to make sure the screen door was tightly shut. Jenny said it was and called a belated thanks. Then she and Lauren ran down to the bay to look for Finder. As usual he was wading in the shallows, and when he saw the two girls, he splashed quickly out of the water. Then they returned to the beach and started toward Mariners Haven, walking next to the surf where the footing was firmer and the sand cooler. Finder stayed close to them much of the time, although occasionally he would wander toward the dunes to hunt through the wheat-colored beach grass. The further they walked, the more improbable it seemed to Jenny that they would see anything. She guessed that they must be almost even with the gray house, but there was no sign of anyone on the beach.

"Should we look for a path?" Lauren asked.

"We might as well."

Turning away from the surf, the girls walked up to the dunes and began to search. At first they were unable to find anything that looked like a path, but Finder soon showed them where one was by turning into it. When it looked as if he might keep going, Jenny called to him. The dog stopped and hesitated, then turned back reluctantly.

"That must be the path."

Lauren nodded, pointing out that there were no fresh footprints. "No one's been down to the beach since the rain last night."

"Want to go back?" Jenny asked.

"Let's keep going. I want to see if that girl's here; you know, the one Mom was talking about."

Leaving the path, they returned to the lower part of the beach and continued on their way. Mariners Haven was very much like their own community, but bigger. Jenny didn't know many people who lived there, but she had heard her father say that it was a family community, and there were always a number of children on the beach. As they walked past, they saw many family groups, the children running back and forth between their parents and the surf. Once a little boy threw a ball that came bouncing toward Jenny's feet, and she picked it up and threw it back. The boy had a sister of about her age, and Jenny was hoping she would speak to them, but the girl turned away without appearing to notice them. Then a short while later two boys, who were playing in the surf, tried to splash them, and she and Lauren retreated to the upper part of the beach.

When they came to the west-end walk, they turned to the right and climbed the steps to the top of the dune line.

"Which is your friend's house?" Jenny asked.

"The green one at the end of the walk."

They walked quickly to the house. Lauren's friend

was sunbathing on the deck and was delighted to see Lauren, and the three girls returned to the beach and spent the next two hours swimming, sunning, and playing paddle-tennis. When Jenny and Lauren finally left, it was early afternoon. Returning to the beach, they crossed quickly to the edge of the surf, strolling at a relaxed pace and chatting about their visit. They had almost reached the eastern end of Mariners Haven when, interrupting Jenny in mid-sentence, Lauren whispered that the men and the boy were up ahead.

Jenny looked quickly. Two men were standing well back on the beach, watching a boy of ten or eleven, who was playing in the sand below them. As Jenny looked, Finder spotted the group and raced ahead, running headlong toward the boy. At first the men didn't see him. When they did, one of them took the surprised boy by the arm, pulling him to his feet, while the other ran forward to stand between the boy and the onrushing dog. In spite of this, the boy saw Finder and called to him. Immediately the man who was holding the boy spoke to him sharply, jerking his arm, while the other man, who was almost bald, tried to intercept Finder with a kick. It was a close thing, and only Finder's agility saved him. In mid-stride he managed to slither to one side. Then he came to a stop, watching the group before him.

The boy was crying now and struggling to get loose from the man who was holding him. Jenny and Lauren edged closer, but something about the two men made them hesitate to come too close. The bald man, who was standing between Finder and the boy, said something to the other man, but Jenny was unable to understand the words and guessed that he was speaking a foreign language. After a brief consultation, the bald man spoke to the boy, apparently giving him an order, which the boy protested in a high, shrill voice. This time Jenny was sure that he was not speaking English.

All this time Finder had remained frozen in place, but now he began to steal forward, his eyes never leaving the boy and the two men. Jenny held her breath as she watched him, and she felt Lauren grip her arm tightly. Abruptly Finder leaped forward, and the boy tried to bend down to reach him, but the men were too quick for them. While one man jerked the boy erect, the other caught Finder with a vicious kick that sent him sprawling. He got up immediately, snarling at the man, but the man had picked up a piece of driftwood and stood in front of the boy, brandishing it menacingly. It was all Jenny could do not to dash to Finder's assistance; it was only her fear of the men that kept her from it.

The man who was holding the stick was watching them now, and Jenny guessed that he was unsure what to do. Then he turned, and speaking to the man who was holding the boy, he motioned toward the dunes. As the boy was spun around, he shouted something to the girls, but whether because of language or distance, Jenny was unable to understand what he said. In any case the bald man spoke sharply to him, and he did not speak again as the three of them returned to the path that Finder had run up earlier.

Finder followed them at first, but the bald men was watching and threatened him with the stick. Before he could resume his trailing, Jenny had him, and she held him tightly. She didn't want him to be tied up and beaten again, and after seeing the men, she had no doubt that they had been the ones who had tied him up originally. Finally Finder began to calm down, and Jenny picked him up and carried him until they were far enough down the path that she felt she could safely put him down. Even then she kept a close eye on him.

On the way back she and Lauren talked over what had happened. Lauren thought that the boy was being held prisoner by the two men, and she was all for doing something about it. Jenny was inclined to agree with her, but pointed out that even if they were right, there was little they could do except to tell an adult.

"Maybe we can help the boy escape," Lauren suggested.

"From those two men?" Jenny shook her head. "They know about us now. We'd better be careful. Did you see the way that bald man was looking at us?"

"He gave me the creeps," Lauren agreed. "He looked just like the mummy that had come back to life in a horror movie I saw on television one time. Do you think he's Egyptian?"

"He might be. He and the other man both had dark hair, and they were dark-looking. How old do you think the boy is?"

"I don't know. He seems to be around Billy's age, or maybe younger. He looks Egyptian, too."

"He probably is." Jenny glanced back to make sure

Finder was with them. Then she turned to Lauren. "Let's tell Mr. Pritchard what happened."

"He might not like it."

"Might not like what?"

"Didn't he tell us to stay away from the people if we saw them?"

"We did stay away from them."

Lauren glanced at Jenny and shrugged. "Don't say I didn't warn you."

Turning up from the beach, Jenny called Finder, and he ran along behind them as they made their way to Mr. Pritchard's house. The old man was sitting on his porch, smoking a pipe, and he showed no surprise when he saw them, leaning down to scratch Finder, who was sniffing his trousers.

"You've been to Mariners Haven I take it," he observed, stretching his feet out in front of him and settling back in his chair. "See anything?"

"We saw a lot."

Without waiting for further invitation, Jenny told him what had happened. When she had finished, he was silent for some time. Then he got to his feet and stepped inside, telling them to wait. When he returned, he had three glasses in one hand and a can of Coca-Cola in the other. Setting down his own glass, which was half-full, he filled the other two glasses with Coke and passed them to the girls. Then he sat down and began to sip his drink.

"I'll tell you the way it looks to me," he said finally. "From everything you've told me, I think it's a safe assumption that your dog there belongs to this boy you saw on the beach. Now, for some reason the men with the boy don't want him to have the dog. They probably chased it away once, and they've kept it away."

"How about when they tied Finder up?" Jenny asked.

"We have no way of knowing why they did that. Maybe they were intending to take him to the mainland and turn him loose, only he got away."

"Do you think they're holding the boy against his will?" Lauren asked.

"I wouldn't want to speculate on that. There's no way of telling. I think it's a possibility, but there's no proof of it."

"Why did the man have to hold him then, and why did he threaten to hit him?"

"He wanted to keep him away from the dog, didn't he?"

"Why would he want to do that?"

"Who knows?" Mr. Pritchard took a final sip of his drink and put the empty glass on the table next to him. "For all we know, one of the men could be the boy's father. Maybe the dog bit him or someone else, and he made up his mind to get rid of it."

"Finder wouldn't bite anybody. He isn't the kind of dog that bites people. He didn't even bite the man who kicked him."

"All right. Maybe the man doesn't like dogs. What I'm saying is there's no way to know. There might be something funny about all this, but the chances are ten to one it's nothing more than a man who's decided to get rid of his son's dog, and his son doesn't like it."

"I don't think either of those men was the boy's father," Jenny observed quietly

"You may *think* that, but you don't *know*. If I were you, I'd forget the whole thing."

"What if the boy was kidnapped?" Lauren asked.

"Kidnapped! Where did you get that wild idea?"

"It looked to me like he was a prisoner."

"It may have looked that way, but that doesn't mean it was that way. If the boy was kidnapped, they'd be keeping him in the house under lock and key. They wouldn't be taking him to the beach where he could yell to someone for help."

"How can he yell for help if he doesn't speak English?"

Mr. Pritchard shook his head. "You two are bound and determined to make this a capital offense, aren't you? All right, let's get this straight. All you know is that the boy's dog has been chased away because the men don't want it around, and the boy isn't happy about it. That isn't enough to tell the police or anyone else. Additionally you don't like the look of the two men, and you have a feeling that the boy is a prisoner. That's your opinion; no more and no less. Finally, we guess that the men are foreigners, maybe Egyptians. It's no crime to be a foreigner. In other words, you haven't found out anything of substance. There's probably a perfectly simple explanation for the whole thing."

"Don't you think it's suspicious, though?"

Mr. Pritchard picked up his glass, saw it was empty, and put it down again. "Yes, I do think there are some grounds for suspicion," he admitted cautiously. "In fact, I intend to speak to a couple of friends from the old days when I go into New York. *But . . .*" and as he spoke the word, he fixed them both with the full force of his glance, "I don't want you or any of the other kids in this community to go near the gray house. Is that clear?"

"You think we may be right then?"

"On the contrary, I think you're wrong. I'll go further than that. I'm almost positive you're wrong. But that doesn't mean I want you to take chances."

The girls nodded.

"You better get along now."

"Will you tell us what you find out from your friends?"

Mr. Pritchard leaned back in his chair. "It all depends on what they tell me." He winked at Jenny and smiled. "Now scat."

10 Jenny Takes a Chance

THE next week seemed to creep by. Jenny was anxious to learn more about the gray house and its occupants. So long as the mystery of the boy and the two men remained unresolved, she could not be sure that she would be able to keep Finder. It was a dark cloud hanging constantly on her horizon, and there seemed to be no way to remove it. Her parents had forbidden her to go to the gray house; and Mr. Pritchard, the only one who knew anything, didn't even want to talk about it.

Finally at the end of the week, matters came to a head. She and Lauren were standing on the Reids' deck late in the morning when Lauren spotted the cabin

66

cruiser anchoring off the trail to the gray house. They continued to watch, using Lauren's binoculars, and a few minutes later they saw the two men and the boy row out from the beach in the dory. When they reached the cabin cruiser, they climbed aboard, and the dory was tied to the stern. Then the cruiser lifted anchor and sailed away.

"The gray house should be empty now," Lauren commented, giving Jenny a quick look.

"I guess so," Jenny agreed, continuing to watch the boat through the glasses. She knew what Lauren was thinking. If they were going to go to the gray house, now was the time to do it. She was tempted. After all, if the house was in fact deserted, no one need ever know that she had gone there. But that was a big *if:* a scary *if*.

"What are you going to do?"

Jenny put down the glasses. In that instant her mind was made up, but she was careful not to let Lauren know. If she was going to do it, she intended to do it alone. Shrugging her shoulders, she got to her feet, saying that so long as no one was there, there would be nothing to see at the gray house anyway. Lauren looked at her suspiciously, but said nothing. Calling Finder, Jenny made an excuse and wandered off toward the bay, turning west when she reached the shore. Fortunately there was no one in sight, and she quickened her pace, passing her own and Bachelors Walk, and moving rapidly down the shore until she reached the path that led to the gray house. Looking to all sides to be sure she was not being watched or followed, she called Finder and turned inland.

The closer she came to the gray house, the more Jenny began to worry. She kept asking herself what she would do if someone were there, and she couldn't come up with a really good answer. Finally she decided that it would be best to pretend that she was taking a walk, and that when her dog had turned into the path, she had followed him. After all, it could have happened that way.

Reaching the clearing in which the gray house was nestled, Jenny stopped while Finder hurried forward to nose around the yard. She remained motionless for some time, studying the house and listening for any sound of movement. Finally, finished with his inspection, Finder turned to her and barked. She watched him, but still she did not move, waiting to see if his barking would bring anyone out. At last, reassured by the continuing silence, she crossed the yard, and climbing the steps to the back porch, she peered through the window in the back door. Although the shade had been drawn, it had not been closed all the way, and she had a good view of the kitchen.

The first thing she noticed were the dirty dishes. They were piled in the sink and on the counter, and this worried her because it suggested that either someone was still in the house, or that the men and the boy expected to return very shortly. She looked back at Finder, who was watching her attentively. She assumed that he would bark were someone to approach, but she was still very uneasy. Turning back to the house, she moved from window to window the length of the porch, trying to find another window with the shade up. Unsuccessful in this, she returned to the back door and looked in again. Opposite her there was an interior door, which apparently led to the living room. Craning her neck to see more, she put her left hand on the doorknob, and to her surprise, it began to turn and the latch clicked open.

For several seconds Jenny stood motionless, staring at the half-open door. Up to this moment it hadn't occurred to her to enter the house, but now that the door stood open in front of her, it seemed a bit of luck too good to pass up. If she were going to learn about the boy and the two men, now was the time. Perhaps if she had taken long enough to think it through, Jenny would have closed the door and walked away, but she wasn't thinking clearly. Everything was happening too fast for that. She gave Finder one quick look. Then she stepped inside, closing the door behind her, and crossed the kitchen to the interior door.

The living room in which she found herself was quite large. There were two unmade cots on the west wall, and here she guessed the two men slept. In the center of the east wall was a fireplace with a couch and two chairs set comfortably around it, and on the north wall, a bar. She moved silently toward the fireplace. Although she was positive no one was in the house, she was still uneasy.

She had reached the fireplace now, and she bent down to look at the magazines on the table. Most of them were old copies of *Life, Time,* and *Sports Illustrated,* but on the sofa she found two more recent magazines. She glanced through them quickly. They were written in the same language as the newspaper they had found under the house, and there were pictures of pyramids and ancient jewelry. Putting the magazines back where she had found them, Jenny stepped into the next room.

There was a bed on one side. Next to it was a table, and across from it a bureau and chair. From the toys scattered around, Jenny guessed that the boy slept here. She looked at the toys carefully, but there was nothing unusual about them, except for one book that was in the language of the magazines and had pictures of camels, turbaned men, and palm trees. Getting up from the floor, she looked on top of the bureau. There was a thermometer near the edge, and behind it a bottle of cough syrup and a tin of aspirin tablets. She stepped forward, intending to pick up the thermometer, but her hand never reached the bureau.

A loud barking outside the house momentarily froze her in place. Then she raced for the back door. Pulling it open, she took a quick look and slipped out, closing the door behind her. Finder was barking at the entrance to the trail that led up from the bay. She started to call him, but changing her mind, ran to the beach side of the clearing and jumped behind a large clump of bushes. Here she stopped to catch her breath, her eyes glued to the break in the shrubbery opposite her. Finder was still barking excitedly, but Jenny noticed that his tail was wagging. She watched him, puzzled. Then she heard a voice, and she almost burst out laughing. Seconds later Lauren and Billy strolled into the clearing, trying hard to look as if they just happened to be walking by. When they saw Finder and Jenny, they were astonished, and Jenny quickly told them what she had done and described the interior of the house.

"Do you think the boy is sick?" Billy asked when she had finished.

"He could be. Maybe that's why they went off."

Billy leaned down to stroke Finder. "Think they'll be back?"

"I think so," Jenny replied. "The way they left everything, it looks like they're planning to come back."

After leaving the gray house, the three of them walked to the beach. It was a slightly overcast day with a strong southeast wind, and the surf was heavy. Finder immediately galloped to the water's edge and ran along it, looking through the debris that had been washed up. Billy and the girls followed more slowly, talking about the gray house and its occupants. At first they were inclined to tell Mr. Pritchard what they had seen, but they decided against it. Under the circumstances, the less said to adults, the better. They were almost back to their own stretch of beach when Billy stopped abruptly, pointing out over the water.

"Look at the birds!" he exclaimed.

Squinting their eyes against the glare, the girls looked where he was pointing. A cloud of gulls was wheeling and swooping far out over the water.

"Are they diving?" Jenny asked.

"It looks like it. There must be fish under them."

The three of them watched for some time. Then Lauren and Jenny left the beach, returning to Lauren's house where they spent the afternoon. Jenny was in good spirits when she returned to her house, but her spirits were dampened half an hour later at supper.

"I've got something to tell you," her father announced suddenly, turning to her. "I've been talking to Bill Sargeant. I told him about our problem of what to do with Finder at the end of the summer. To make a long story short, he said he'd be glad to keep Finder for us this winter. We can pick him up when we're ready to come here again next summer, and of course, we can visit him anytime we want to. The Sargeants are good with animals, and they'll take excellent care of Finder. I think it's a pretty good solution."

Jenny stared down at her plate. She knew her father wanted a response, but she was too angry and shocked to give him one. It was Billy who voiced what she was thinking by observing that given a choice, he was sure Finder would rather stay with them than with the Sargeants, even if it did mean living in New York.

"No way," Mr. Martin said firmly. "I don't intend to have a dog in our New York City apartment, and that's that. This way we'll have Finder again next summer, and we can see him whenever we want to in between. It seems to me it makes sense."

As he said this, he turned to Jenny, but she had had enough. Getting up from the table, she ran into her own room with Finder at her heels and closed the door. She half-expected her father to call her back to the table, but he didn't. When the others went to bed two hours later, she was still awake, lying on her back, staring up at the ceiling.

11 Fish!

During breakfast the next morning Jenny spoke as little as possible. She ate quickly, excusing herself as soon as she was finished. She was eager to tell Lauren what had happened, but to her surprise, Lauren was less sympathetic than she had expected.

"You knew your father didn't want to have a dog," Lauren observed, "so I don't know why you're so surprised. I think he's being pretty fair."

"Fair!" Jenny exclaimed. "Do you think it's fair for the Sargeants to have Finder for nine months and me for just three?"

"It won't be that way. Your family's moving out of the city next year. You told me so yourself."

"I'd like to see you if it was *your* dog who was being given away. You'd be yelling and screaming."

"He's not being given away. He's just being farmed out for a few months."

It was Lauren at her most logical, and it made Jenny furious. Turning away, she stamped off in a rage and walked out to the beach. For the next hour she sat watching the surf. She was still sitting there with Finder curled at her feet, when her father appeared and sat down beside her. They did not speak for some time. Then her father asked if she had seen any sign of fish.

Jenny shook her head.

"I was talking to Gus Kovack yesterday," he observed. "He has a friend who fishes commercially. He says the sardines are massing up along the South Shore, and the bluefish are beginning to find them. We should be getting fish any day now."

"We saw a flock of birds off the outer bar yesterday," Jenny told him.

"Were they working?"

"Just about the way those birds are now."

Jenny pointed to a small flock of gulls that were swooping and diving off to their left, and she and her father studied them, shading their eyes against the sun.

"Looks like they're over fish," he concluded. "Tell me, Jen, now that you've had a chance to think about it, do you like my idea of boarding Finder with the Sargeants any better?"

Jenny had been expecting the question, and she was ready for it.

"I don't see why it would be so much trouble to have Finder in New York," she replied, keeping her eyes on the water. "Billy and I would be the ones who would walk him and feed him and all that stuff. Finder wouldn't bother you at all."

"It's not a question of Finder *bothering* me. It's just that a dog like Finder loves to run and hunt, and he can't do that in New York."

"It would only be for one winter."

"We *think* it would be for one winter. We just can't be sure. Look, Jen, I don't want an animal in New York. I can understand your finding that difficult to accept, but that's the way I feel. All right. Since Finder can't come to New York with us, we have to find some other place for him to go. Can you think of any place better than the Sargeants'? If you can, I'll be happy to consider it."

Jenny shook her head. "No, but I still think Billy's right. If you were to give Finder his choice, he'd rather stay with us, even if he did have to live in New York City. I don't think you're being fair to him."

"Maybe I'm not, but that's the way it's going to be." Mr. Martin stood up and stretched. "I think I'll go for a swim. Want to join me?"

Jenny shook her head, her eyes once more on the spot far out where the birds were working. Mr. Martin stood for a moment. Then he turned and walked to the surf. Jenny was still sitting on the sand, staring out over the water when he returned from his dip. He hesitated, as if about to stop, then left the beach.

Jenny watched off and on for much of that day and

the next; and the day after, she and Ron and Billy watched together, but although they frequently saw birds, the fish did not cross the outer bar. Friday the fish finally came in. Jenny had been at Lauren's house when the Sargeants' bell sounded, announcing that the blitz was on. Jenny ran home to get her surf rod, and minutes later, she was sprinting to the beach. The sight that greeted her when she reached the dune line was one for which she had been waiting all summer. The air out in front of the community was dense with birds, wheeling just above the water and diving to the surface to catch the sardines that were skipping madly in their efforts to escape the hungry fish below. Mr. Kovack and Mr. Parks were already fighting fish, and off to the left she could see the Reids rushing across the beach, followed closely by Ron and his father.

"Come on!" she yelled to Billy who was just behind her with his new rod, and the two of them raced to the water's edge, casting their plugs the moment they arrived. To Jenny's relief, her cast sailed true. She gave it a jerk, and the water erupted under it. She could feel the shock all the way to her heels as the rod bent and the reel released line in an anguished squeal. The fish was heavy, and it ran strongly for a moment. Then it was off. The drag had been too loose.

Without reeling in the line, Jenny tightened the drag and then began to retrieve her plug. Out of the corner of her eye, she could see that her father and Billy both had fish on. She glanced quickly in the other direction, wondering if the twins were fishing, but before she was able to spot them, her line came taut and her rod bent. She struck automatically, and this time, although the fish battled strongly, she was able to control it. Minutes later she had the fish on the beach. It was a bluefish of roughly three pounds. Luckily the plug popped free of its own accord, and tossing her catch well back on the sand, Jenny cast again. To her left she could see that Billy either had on a new fish or the same fish he had been fighting earlier, and on the right she could see Skip and Ron both fighting fish. She watched her own plug carefully, but there was no strike. The birds had moved further out, following the baitfish, and they were now almost at the limit of her casting range.

Pulling her plug back through the break, she reeled until the wire leader was just short of the rod tip. Then she swung the rod back over her shoulder and brought it forward in a long, graceful arc. The plug sailed through the air, and to her delight, it landed much further out than she had ever been able to cast it before. She waited a fraction of a second and then gave her plug a jerk. Again she waited, and again she jerked it. Five jerks later it happened. The plug disappeared in a shower of foam. Jenny struck firmly, and she knew instantly that she had hooked something far bigger than she had ever had on her line before. The fish took line slowly but steadily, and there was nothing she could do to stop it.

"You've got a big one. Take it slow and easy. Keep the pressure on, but don't force it."

Her father was standing just to her left, his own rod held loosely by his side as he watched.

"It's taking an awful lot of line," she said nervously.

"They always do on the first run. Just stay with it."

The fish was running toward her now, and Jenny reeled frantically, trying to keep the line taut. Then it turned, and she could feel an odd vibration on the line.

"I think it's snagged me on something."

"Nothing out there for it to snag you on. It's probably working the plug against the bottom. Just keep the pressure on it."

Suddenly the fish began to move down the shore in a dogged, steady run that peeled line from Jenny's reel.

"Better follow it," Mr. Martin advised. "It's using the undertow."

Jenny moved down the shore, staying even with the fish, while her father followed. The others had all stopped fishing and were watching, aware that Jenny had hooked something very large.

"Do you think it's a striper?" Jenny asked over her shoulder.

"Probably."

The fish had stopped now and had settled to a punishing nose-to-bottom resistance, using its weight to contest every inch of line. Jenny's arms were aching from the effort of holding the rod vertically against the pull of the line, and she had a moment of wondering whether she would be able to hold out.

"Getting tired?"

The question had the effect of rekindling her determination. The fish was close now, and Billy and Ron had moved to the surf's edge, while her father readied the hand gaff. Suddenly she saw the fish for the first time. It was huge; fully three feet long, its gold and black stripes glowing in the roll of the wave.

"It's bigger than Finder!" Jenny gasped.

"Heck, it's bigger than Rex!" Ron corrected her.

The fish was almost in reach now, and Mr. Martin waded out to be ready to gaff it.

"Careful," he called tensely. "Don't force it. It might have a last run left in it."

One last turn of the reel; that's all it would take. One last turn . . . and then it was over. The line suddenly went slack. Jenny almost fell over backwards, her eyes staring at the long, golden-white shape rolling in the wave. Her father lunged desperately with the gaff, but the fish was sinking out of sight, and he couldn't reach it. A second more they saw it. Then it was gone.

The next thing Jenny knew, her father had an arm around her shoulders. Slowly they stepped back from the surf. There was nothing to say. Billy picked up the plug and looked at it, letting out a soft whistle.

"It straightened the hook," he announced.

Sure enough, one of the barbs of the rear treble hook had been straightened.

"That's tough luck," Mr. Martin commented, turning the plug over in his fingers. "There's nothing you could do about it. That happens with a big fish."

"How big do you think it was?" Jenny asked.

Mr. Martin shook his head. "It's hard to say. I'd guess it was over thirty pounds, maybe more. It was bigger than anything I've ever hooked."

"Do you think I put too much pressure on it?"

"You did just right."

By this time everybody had gathered around, and they were all exclaiming over the size of the fish, passing Jenny's plug from hand to hand. Tired as she was, Jenny felt a warm glow of pride and satisfaction that helped to soothe the pang of disappointment. To have come so close was hard, but at least everyone had seen the fish, and that made it better. Turning to Billy, she asked how many he had caught.

"I caught two and lost one other. Daddy got a big one."

"How big?" Jenny asked, turning to her father.

"About eight pounds. It was a striper. I guess they were picking up after the bluefish."

"I got a blue before. It's over there somewhere."

"I already picked it up," Billy told her. "I thought it was one of mine."

They continued to talk for some time after that, comparing notes on the fish caught and missed. Although Jenny enjoyed the conversation, she was relieved when her father suggested they go back to the house for lunch. She was both tired and thirsty.

When they returned to the house, lunch was ready, and they sat down at the table. Finder was stretched out at Jenny's feet where he would be ready if any food happened to fall to the floor. He had gone off with Rex earlier in the morning and had not appeared on the beach until after the fishing was over. As Billy got up from the table, he made a sign to Jenny to meet him on the back deck.

"Guess what?" he said as soon as she had approached close enough to hear his whisper. "The boat came back this morning, and one of the men and the boy rowed to shore."

"Which man?" Jenny asked.

"I was too far away to tell."

Jenny considered for a moment, looking down at Finder. She was tired, and she had been intending to take a nap. On the other hand, Billy's news intrigued her.

"Let's go over to Ron's house," she said finally.

Billy grinned. That was what he had been hoping she would say.

12 Encounter

Ron was not at his house, so Billy and Jenny walked down to the West Walk dock, where Ron and his father had gone to fillet the fish they had caught that morning. When this job was finished, Mr. Rollins returned to the house with the tray of fillets, while Ron remained with Jenny and Billy.

"What time is it?" Ron asked as soon as his father had left.

"About two o'clock. Have you seen Lauren?"

"She's coming now."

Turning, Jenny saw Lauren walking along the shore in their direction. She waved, and Lauren waved back.

Moments later she joined them, sitting down next to Jenny.

"Who wants to walk to the gray house?" Jenny asked abruptly.

Ron turned to look at her. "I thought the gray house was off limits."

"It is. I just thought we'd take a walk and use the path as a short cut to the beach. We can leave the dogs home."

Ron whistled softly, but said nothing. It was Lauren who put into words what they were all thinking.

"Mr. Pritchard told us to stay away from the gray house, Jenny."

"I know that."

"What if the men and the boy are there?"

"They are there."

Lauren stared at her, shaking her head. "You're crazy."

"No I'm not. Look at it this way. If we're going to find out anything about the men and the boy, we've got to start now."

"Why do we have to find out anything about them?" Ron asked.

"What if they're holding the boy prisoner? What if they kidnapped him?"

"Are you serious?"

"Ask Lauren."

Ron glanced at Lauren, and then back at Jenny. "What do you figure to do?"

"I just want to walk by the house. People must walk up that path all the time. It's like Mr. Pritchard said.

Who's going to get mad at a bunch of kids?"

"So what if we walk by the house? What good will that do?"

"We might see something."

"What if Mr. Pritchard or your father finds out?"

"How are they going to find out? Are you going to tell them?"

"You know what I think?" Billy interrupted suddenly. "I think we should take Skip with us, and maybe the twins."

"Why?"

"Because it might be hard for us to act naturally, but it would be easy for Skip and the twins, since they don't know anything."

"How will we get them to go?" Lauren asked.

"We'll think of something."

They talked a few minutes more. Then, leaving the dogs at Ron's house, they walked to the Sargeants' to look for Skip, only to find that he had gone to the mainland for a dentist appointment.

"I guess that leaves the twins," Ron said disgustedly as they set off in search of Ty and Win. They found them next to the Bachelors Walk dock. Jenny told them that she and the others were walking to Mariners Haven and asked if they would like to come along.

"Why walk there?" Ty asked.

"We're trying to find something," Jenny replied.

Ty and Win exchanged a quick look. Because they were forever playing tricks on the others, they were never sure who might be holding a grudge against them, and they were always afraid of a trap. Two days before, Ty had slipped a crab into Billy's clam bucket, and it had given Billy a good nip. Billy had ducked him in revenge, but Ty wasn't sure that Billy might not be planning some further revenge.

"What are you looking for?" he asked.

"We're trying to find a notebook that Mr. Ketchum said he lost on one of his walks. He said he'd give a five dollar reward to anyone who found it."

Now as it happened, this was true. Mr. Ketchum had lost a notebook the day before, and he had told Billy and Ron that he would give a reward to the finder. Of course, he had been walking on the Pirates Cove side of Mid Station when he had lost it, but Jenny didn't mention this. The twins were again looking at one another, and Jenny knew that she almost had them.

"You two are pretty good at finding things, and we know where he was walking. We figured we could look for it together and split the reward."

"Why don't you look for it yourselves?" Win asked quickly.

"We already have. We couldn't find it."

For a moment the twins were silent. Then Win asked why if she and Ty found it they should split the reward.

"How are you going to find it unless you know where he was walking? You can't ask him because he went to the mainland for the day."

That clinched it. Exchanging a final glance, the twins agreed to go with them, and they set off toward Mariners Haven. They had gone no more than fifty yards, however, when Ty came to a halt.

"Did he walk here?" he asked.

"Why do you think we're walking here if he didn't?" Ron asked in return.

"We should be looking then."

Ty retraced his steps, searching the ground carefully. Then he jogged back to them, and he and Win began to search the ground as they went along, the others walking in a group behind them and also pretending to search.

"Was it low tide when he was walking here?" Win asked a few yards further on.

"I don't know," Billy responded. "I think it was about mid-tide."

"If it were low tide and he was walking below the high-water mark, the notebook would have floated away when the tide came in."

"Or it would have gotten all wet," Ty added. "I think it's a wild goose chase anyway."

"You didn't have to come," Ron put in quickly.

"We asked him to come," Jenny countered, giving Ron a quick look before turning to Ty. "It's two dollars and fifty cents, Ty. That would buy a fishing plug."

"Who wants a fishing plug?"

"It's still two-fifty. You and Win can spend it on anything you like."

They had almost reached the cross-island path that led to the gray house, and Jenny was already considering how she would manage things. To get the twins on the path would be no problem. It was what they would do once they got to the house that was troubling her, and she could feel an uneasy fluttering in her stomach. Fortunately, the twins were far too involved in the search to notice her uneasiness.

When they came to the path, Jenny turned into it, saying that this was the path Mr. Ketchum had taken. The twins didn't question the information, but moved ahead of her along the narrow path like a pair of bloodhounds, their backs bent and their eyes fixed on the ground. Seconds later, Ron, who was walking just behind Jenny, put a hand on her arm and pointed ahead. They were coming to the clearing. The group moved forward slowly, the twins in the lead and the others following. As they emerged from the shadow of the bushes, Jenny had to shade her eyes against the glare of the sun. Ty had stopped and was staring at the gray house.

"How long's that house been here?" he asked.

"I don't know," Jenny replied, keeping her voice low. "I guess it's been here a long time."

"Let's look at it."

This was exactly what Jenny was hoping he would say, and she quickly agreed. They moved forward, and after looking at the rear of the house, they circled to the front. Here they had a surprise in store for them. The boy whom Jenny and Lauren had seen earlier was playing at the foot of the front steps. Evidently he had not heard them, because he looked up, startled, as they came around the corner, and jumped to his feet. At the same time a dark, heavyset man stepped out of the house and joined the boy. For a moment the man, the boy, and the six children stared at one another. Then

Ty stepped forward. The boy had been playing with a tractor, and Ty wanted to look at it. He had crossed half the distance to where the boy was standing, when the man jerked the boy by the arm, almost throwing him back up the steps. Then he stepped toward the astonished Ty.

"Go!" he demanded in heavily accented English, pointing toward the path, where it left the clearing to go to the beach.

Now if it had been anyone but Ty, the thing would have ended right there, but Ty had a temper to match his flaming red hair, and he was afraid of no one. Facing the man, he planted his feet firmly and stood his ground. The man stared at him. It had evidently never occurred to him that a nine-year-old boy might choose to defy him.

"Go!" he repeated once more, pointing to the path.

"Why should I?" Ty muttered sullenly.

Again he and the man were silent. Watching them, Jenny almost forgot to breathe. She could not have moved if she had wanted to. Suddenly the man rushed at Ty. At the same instant, Ty jumped to one side and kicked the man sharply on the shin as he went past, causing him to stumble and fall. Before the man could get to his feet, Ty had gained the path to the beach, and the others followed him closely, running as fast as their legs could carry them. Only when they reached the safety of the open beach and were assured that the man was not following did they slow to a walk, but they did not talk for several seconds. They were breathing too hard for that.

Finally Ron put a hand on Ty's shoulder, staring at him with new respect. "Ty," he said, "you're crazy! I would have taken off so fast when that guy told me to go you wouldn't have seen my dust. What made you stand there?"

"I don't know," Ty replied. "I guess I just didn't feel like moving."

For the next few minutes they talked excitedly about what had happened, and there was no question that Ty was the hero of the occasion. He walked next to Ron, and Win walked to his left, while the others grouped around them. Presently the conversation turned to the boy and why the man had acted as he had.

"I didn't like that man," Win observed. "He was really rough with the boy."

"He was," Jenny agreed, turning to Ron. "What do you think about what I was saying before, Ron? Does it still sound crazy to you?"

"Maybe not," Ron admitted.

Ty looked up quickly. "What were you saying before?"

Seeing the others exchange a rapid glance, he stopped, his face coloring and his pale blue eyes fixed on them. "Hey, what's going on here?" he asked.

"It was something I told Ron," Jenny hedged.

"What did you tell him?"

"I'll tell you about it when we get back."

"You promise?" Ty looked at her doubtfully. He knew that they were trying to keep something from him.

Jenny nodded. "I promise."

When they returned to Mid Station, they went quickly to Ron's house to pick up the dogs. They could have stayed at the house since Ron's parents were away, but instead they walked down to the bay and sat in a semicircle to the left of the dock. The dogs had run off as soon as they were let out of the house, and they could hear them barking over toward Bachelors Walk.

"All right. Tell me what you were talking about before," Ty demanded as soon as they were seated, and Jenny gave him and Win a quick summary of all that had happened. The twins listened closely, and only when she had finished did Win ask if Mr. Ketchum had really lost a notebook. Jenny nodded, hoping that they would not learn that she had tricked them. Fortunately, Ty was much too interested in what she had told him to care about Mr. Ketchum's notebook.

"Do you really think they're holding him prisoner?" he asked.

Jenny nodded.

"Why don't we rescue him?"

"How?" Billy asked.

"All we have to do is to tell him to come with us."

"How can we? He doesn't speak English."

"He'd understand."

"What about the man?"

"He could have gotten away from him this afternoon. The man's slow."

"How do you know the boy would have come with us? He didn't try to run to us, did he?"

Ty looked at Billy, shaking his head slowly. "What

do you think we should do then?" he asked.

This time it was Billy's turn to shake his head. "I don't know. I just think we have to be careful."

"It's been a month now," Jenny reminded them, "and we haven't done a thing yet. I think Ty's got a point. I think it's up to us to do something."

"What?"

"I don't know. Maybe if we watch them, we can think of something."

"You mean spy on them?" Ty asked.

"That's it!" Lauren exclaimed excitedly. "That's what we should do. If we spy on them, maybe we can find some way to signal the boy."

"How can we do that if the boy can't speak English?" Ron objected. "Heck, if he could run away, he would have run away long ago."

"I still think we should watch them," Lauren argued. "Maybe if we watch them, we can find some way to get close to the boy. Then maybe he can tell us who he is."

"He can't speak English, dumb-dumb!" Ron exclaimed.

"I don't mean that. I mean maybe he could pass us a message."

"You mean in writing?" Ron asked.

"If he doesn't speak it, he has to write it, doesn't he, dumb-dumb?"

Lauren stuck out her tongue at Ron, a gesture that left him very red in the face. He glanced at Jenny, pretending to ignore the laughter of the others.

"Okay. So we're going to spy on them. How?"

Jenny had been thinking while the others were talking, and she had an answer ready.

"We could watch the house in shifts; you know, divide the day in parts, and each of us watch for a couple of hours. If we each took two hours, there are six of us, so we could watch for twelve hours."

"How long do you intend to do this?"

"I don't know." Jenny looked at Ron, then turned to Lauren. "It would depend on what we saw, I guess."

"What are we supposed to be looking for?"

"Oh, come on, Ron, don't be such a pain in the neck!" Lauren exclaimed, turning away in disgust.

"I'm not being a pain in the neck! I just don't think you and Jenny know what you're talking about."

"Look," Jenny said patiently, "if we want to help the boy get away, it seems to me we have to find out what the men who are watching him do during the day. For instance, if we were to find that they take a walk after lunch every day, we might be able to think of some way to help him escape. Or maybe they take him to the beach, or let him play outside the house in the afternoon, or something like that. We won't know unless we watch. Does that make sense?"

Ron had to admit that it did.

"What if they see us watching them?" Billy asked.

"They won't."

"But what if they do?"

"We'll stop watching for a while. I don't think it will be that hard."

"Jenny's right," Win chimed in quickly. "When we were walking by the house today, I noticed there's a high dune with a lot of beach plum on it a little ways to the east. We could watch from there."

"If you can see them, they can see you," Ron objected.

Win shook her head. "The brush is thick up there. If Ty or I were hiding there, nobody would see us."

"How do we get to it?" Lauren asked.

"That's easy," Ty answered. "We can climb the dune from the beach side. Maybe we can use spy glasses.

"We don't need them," Jenny said quickly. "All we want to do is see how often they come out of the house, and whether the men ever leave the boy alone. Does everybody agree that we should watch the house?"

She looked around the circle, and they all nodded.

"Okay. Let's go over to Lauren's house and make out a schedule."

"How will we find the lookout spot?" Billy asked.

"We'll walk over there first thing tomorrow morning, and Ty and Win can show us." Jenny glanced at Ty. "All right?"

The redhead nodded. "I'll show you this afternoon if you want."

"Okay, show us this afternoon."

Getting to her feet, Jenny led the way to Lauren's house. As soon as they were settled in the living room, Lauren pulled out a sheet of paper and a pencil and drew up the list of shifts. Billy suggested that Skip be included, but the others vetoed the suggestion, arguing that they had enough without Skip, and that that would just complicate matters. When the list was completed, Lauren agreed to keep it, and she put it in her room. Then they walked up toward the beach and set off to Mariners Haven to be shown the hiding place.

13 Detectives at Work

Although she did not admit it, Jenny was a little scared that first morning when she started down the beach to relieve Ty. Lauren had agreed to go with her, and the two girls walked next to the surf, trying not to talk about the gray house or the boy. Finally Jenny could restrain herself no longer and asked Lauren point-blank what she thought of the hiding place that Ty had selected.

"It looked good to me," Lauren replied.

"What if someone were to see us? It would be hard to get away."

"Why would anyone see us? Besides, it wouldn't be hard to get away at all. All we have to do is run back down the dune and take the path that goes through the holly grove."

"I still don't like it," Jenny muttered uneasily, kicking at the sand as she walked.

"It was your idea," Lauren reminded her.

"I know. That doesn't make it any better."

When she thought about it, Jenny knew that her plan made sense, but that knowledge didn't help. Two hours of hiding in the bushes seemed very long indeed, and the thought that she would be alone made it worse.

"Look at the birds!" Lauren cried suddenly. Jenny looked where Lauren was pointing. A big flock of gulls was circling and occasionally diving half a mile offshore.

"Wouldn't you know? The darned bluefish will probably come in while I'm lying up there in the bushes, and I'll be the only one who doesn't catch any."

"I won't catch any either."

"That's because you don't like fishing."

Lauren looked at her, shaking her head in mock sympathy.

"Poor, poor Jenny! Everyone's going to have fun but poor, poor Jenny. Let's all go out and eat worms!"

Jenny started to answer back, but caught herself. Instead she gave Lauren a withering stare and walked on, purposely walking faster, so that Lauren had to hustle to keep up with her.

"What's the big hurry?" Lauren asked after a few steps.

"I don't want to keep Ty waiting."

"You've got time. Slow down."

"Why should I?"

"All right, then don't!" Lauren stopped suddenly. Part of Jenny wanted to turn and apologise, but pride wouldn't let her. She was already ten yards down the beach when Lauren called after her.

"Don't ask me to walk down the beach with you again!" Lauren shouted. "I don't have to waste my time on bad-tempered little snots!"

"See if I waste my time on you!" Jenny called back. "Good riddance!"

Jenny walked on. She was angry, and all the more so because she knew that she was in the wrong. And it wasn't just pride; it was selfishness, too. At least that's what her mother had said. *The selfish person thinks only of his own feelings. The generous person thinks of the other person's feelings.* When would she learn to control her temper?

She was level with the dune from which they were to do their watching now, and as she turned away from the surf, her stomach felt suddenly empty, and she had to force herself to go on. When she reached the dune line, she scrambled to the top, running quickly down the other side and across to the foot of the second dune. Ty had seen her coming, and he was already wiggling down the slope. As she came up, he jumped to his feet, his eyes bright and his face flushed.

"Did you see anything?" she whispered.

"Nothing yet. Old Ugly with the bald head came out once and smoked a cigarette on the back porch, but that's all."

"Do you think he saw you?"

"No way!" Ty glanced at her indignantly. "He didn't even look."

They stood for a moment more. Then Ty muttered that he had better be going. He scuffed his bare feet in the sand and glanced back up the slope. Then he turned and walked away, taking a path that led through a holly grove and back toward the bay. Watching him go, Jenny decided that she would take that path in the future and advise others to do the same. Then they wouldn't run the risk of being observed from the beach.

After Ty had disappeared, she got down on all fours and crawled up to the little pocket in the bushes that Ty had hollowed out. She found to her surprise that she could see the gray house clearly in spite of the network of branches and twigs in front of her. She watched carefully at first, but after a while, she let her eyes sweep toward the beach. The birds were still working off Mariners Haven, and she could see a lone fisherman casting into the gray-green swells. He seemed to be fishing with a metal lure, and he retrieved it slowly with long pauses between each jerk.

Abruptly she looked back at the house. A slight movement had caught her eye, and she kept her glance focused on the front steps while she shifted to a more comfortable position. Seconds later the front door opened, and the bald man stepped onto the porch. He stood motionless for almost a minute, his eyes searching the foliage in front of him. For a second he seemed to be looking right at the spot where Jenny was hiding, and she could feel the pulse beating in her wrist where her chin rested against it. Then his glance travelled past, and she let out her breath in relief.

Evidently satisfied with his inspection, the man called over his shoulder, and the boy appeared and walked down the steps with a tractor and a truck cradled under his arms. He started to move away from the house, but the man said something to him, and he stopped abruptly, sat down where he was, and started to play. The man lit a cigarette and leaned back against the railing, watching him. The boy was building a road, pushing the sand out of the way with the tractor and picking it up with the truck. Occasionally he would look at the man, but the man paid little attention to him, smoking one cigarette after another and staring out toward the ocean. Finally he turned and went into the house, and the smaller man, whom Jenny remembered from the beach, took his place. The boy turned and said something to him, and the man nodded and smiled. He was holding a magazine, and he began to leaf through it.

The boy continued to play for more than an hour, which gave Jenny lots of time to study him. He was a good-looking boy in a thin, foreign-seeming way. He had black, curly hair and a narrow, fine-featured face with large eyes. His hands were large, too, with long fingers, and Jenny could tell that he used them well as he manipulated his toys. Indeed, the longer she watched, the more she began to think that he was probably very intelligent. It wasn't any one thing that he did, but rather the way he went about things. It gave her an idea, but before she had time to think about it, the boy stood up in response to a barked command from inside the house, and after shaking the sand out of his toys, walked slowly to the stairs. He looked up at the man on the porch, who shrugged slightly, nodding toward the door in back of him. The boy climbed the stairs and stepped inside. After the boy had gone, the man looked back toward where the boy had been playing. Then he, too, entered the house.

Although Jenny continued to watch, she saw nothing else during the remaining forty minutes of her shift. Now and again she would look toward the surf, but the birds had disappeared, and the fisherman had given up and left the beach. The tide was going out now, and the sun was beating down on the water. Near the center of Mariners Haven, there were several families swimming or lying on the beach, and Jenny wondered whether Lauren's friend might be among them. They had gone back the Saturday after they had seen her, but there had been no sign of her or her family.

"Hey!" came a whispered salutation.

Jenny's heart jumped in her mouth, but then she realized it was only Win coming to relieve her. She crawled down the slope quickly and found Win waiting for her at the bottom.

"Where are they?" Win asked eagerly.

"They're in the house. I think they're eating lunch."

"Good."

"How did you come?" Jenny asked.

"I came through the Holly Grove. Why?"

"That's the way I'm going to tell everyone to come. That way nobody will see us, and there won't be any tracks."

"That's what Ty said. Don't forget to go to Lauren's house so she can write down what happened during your shift."

Jenny nodded, watching Win scramble up the slope. She had forgotten about Lauren. Turning, she started back, thinking about what she would say. Lauren would be expecting an apology. Well, she would get one. After all, like it or not, she had been in the wrong.

When she got back to Mid Station, she found Ron and Billy swimming at the West Walk dock. As soon as they saw her, they asked how it had gone. She told them about watching the boy play. Then she asked if they had seen Lauren.

"She's at her house," Billy answered. "She's mad at you."

"I know."

"Why?"

"None of your business."

Leaving the boys, Jenny walked quickly to the Reid house. To her surprise, Lauren was standing on the front porch, chart in hand, waiting for her. As Jenny came up, she waved a greeting. Jenny waved back, watching her friend carefully, but there was nothing in Lauren's manner to indicate the slightest cloud in their friendship. Answering Lauren's questions, she told her about what she had seen and her impression of the boy, and Lauren wrote it all down on the chart. When she had finished, Lauren put the chart down and stretched.

"I'm sorry about earlier," Jenny said softly. "I just got mad."

"You were scared, that's all."

"I wasn't."

"Sure you were. I will be, too, my first watch."

Jenny tried to object, but Lauren ignored her, quickly changing the subject. When Jenny returned to her own house a few minutes later, she was mad all over again, but she was half-laughing, too. Lauren had evened the score.

Slowly but surely, as Lauren's chart was filled in day after day, they began to learn the routine of the people in the gray house. Generally they would eat breakfast at around eight-thirty or nine. At ten the boy would be allowed to play in the front yard for an hour or so. Then he would be called in, and they would eat lunch at noon. In the early afternoon either the men would let the boy play in the clearing around the house, or if it was a nice day, they would take him to the beach for an hour. Of course, they always watched him closely when he was playing near the house, and if he went to the beach, they would usually both go with him, although on one occasion only the bald man had gone. As a rule, if anyone came close to them on the beach, they would take the boy back to the house, but once they had allowed him to watch a surf fisherman from a distance. After the afternoon play session, they would call the boy inside until five, when they would all go down to the bay. They usually returned fairly promptly, and soon after they would have their supper. The boy never came out after supper, although occasionally one or the other of the men would take a walk on the beach.

By the fifth day everyone was beginning to tire of the business of watching, and at Lauren's suggestion, Jenny called a meeting down by the bay. When everyone was there, she called the meeting to order and went over what they had learned from the report sheet. When she had finished, she asked whether anybody had any ideas.

"I do," Ron said quickly. "As far as I can see, nothing happens during Ty's shift and mine. The boy usually doesn't come out until ten when Jenny's watching, and by the time I come on at six, they've already gone in, so it doesn't seem to me that Ty and I are accomplishing much. What do you think, Ty?"

The redhead nodded. "That's right."

"Now, as far as what they do the rest of the day, I think we have a pretty good line on that."

"Do you mean you don't think we should watch anymore?" Billy asked.

"What good will it do?"

"We've only been watching five days," Jenny objected. "I think we should watch at least three or four more days."

"Why?"

"We might learn something. Besides, I'd like to see if they change anything."

"Like what?"

"Well, for instance, if they keep going to the beach as often."

"They've gone three days out of the five we've watched."

"I'd like to see if they keep on doing that. And another thing. I'd like to know why they walk down to the bay at five o'clock every afternoon."

"I can tell you that," Ty told her. "Just about the time when they go down to the bay, a clam boat usually comes in, and yesterday I saw the guy on the clam boat hand a couple of boxes to Old Ugly."

"What kind of boxes?" Ron asked.

"Groceries, I think, but he probably brings them messages, too."

Ron turned to Jenny. "Well, there's your answer."

"Why don't we watch just during the mornings and afternoons for the next three days?" Lauren suggested. "Then maybe we can try Jenny's plan."

Ty jumped to his feet, eyes fixed on Jenny. "What plan?"

"I don't want to say yet. I want to think about it some more."

"Are you going to try to get the boy away from them?"

"Yes. I mean, if it works, the boy might get away."

"Won't you tell us what you're planning?" Win pleaded.

Jenny shook her head. "Not yet. Just watch for four days, and then I'll tell you."

"Lauren said three."

"I said four," Jenny repeated. "Let's rewrite the

schedule so we're only watching from ten to five. That'll be one hour for each of you and two hours for me."

"That's not fair to you," Billy objected.

"All right. We'll have a different person take the two hour shift each day. How would that be?"

She looked around the circle, but there were no objections, and Lauren took out a new sheet to write down the times and the assignments. Out of the corner of her eye Jenny could see Finder wading in the shallow water, and she called to him. He came on the run, and she reached down to pet him. The last few days had been hard on him and Rex. Since they could not afford to have the dogs following them to the gray house, they had kept them indoors during the hours when Billy, Jenny, or Ron were watching. Finder, particularly, objected to this, and after a morning when they had left him in the Reid house, and he had barked and howled until Mr. Reid finally let him out, they had had to assign someone to stay with the dogs and keep them entertained. Ty and Win thought it a big nuisance, but no one could think of a better way to handle it.

As Jenny stroked Finder, her mind returned again to a question that had been troubling her. If Finder did belong to the boy, and the boy escaped, wasn't he going to want Finder back? Of course he would. It hardly seemed fair, but she could see no way around it. She had tried not to think about it, but it kept popping back into her mind. The others had left, and she and

Lauren were preparing to go when she told Lauren what she was thinking.

"I suppose the boy would want him back," Lauren agreed in response to Jenny's question. "You would."

"That's what I'm thinking."

For some time they were silent. Finally Lauren pointed out that at least now Mr. Martin might be more willing for Jenny to own a dog. Jenny nodded. It was consolation, but it wasn't enough. She looked down at Finder. He was watching her with his habitual *what next* expression. Suddenly she turned to Lauren.

"You know what? I'm going to keep Finder."

"Even if the boy wants him?"

"Even if the boy wants him."

Lauren looked at Jenny. Then she turned away, shaking her head.

"Good luck."

14 Jenny's Plan

THE additional four days of watching turned up nothing new. Three of the days were sunny, and the boy was taken to the beach. The fourth day it rained off and on, and he stayed in the house. Once during this span the clam boat came in with supplies, and on another day, the clammer anchored well out and waded ashore, taking the path up to the house. Fifteen minutes later he returned to his boat. It was Ty who saw him, and he watched until the boat had disappeared before going to Lauren's house to report.

Late in the afternoon of the fourth day they met again on the deck of Lauren's house. Jenny tried to persuade them to watch one more day, but the others voted her down, arguing that they had watched long enough, and that it was time for her to tell them her plan.

"All right," she said finally, "as I see it, the boy isn't going to escape unless we get outside help. The men never let him out of their sight, and if we tried to get him, they'd pull him back in the house before we could say a word.

"What if we found some way of holding them off long enough to give him a chance to run?" Ty asked.

"How could we do that?" Lauren objected. "Remember how fast the bald man got between you and him when we walked by the house that day?"

"He could have run while the man was trying to get me."

"How about the other man?"

"He still could have run."

"But he didn't." Ron glanced at Ty and turned again to Jenny. "He's probably too scared of the men to try to run. I don't blame him. I'll bet that bald man would skin him if he tried to get away."

Jenny nodded. "That's what I think, too. That's why we have to find some other way."

"So what's your plan?" Ty asked impatiently.

"Well, it seems to me that if we can find out *who* the boy is, then we'll know whom to tell. After all, the boy has to come from somewhere, and someone must be looking for him. All we have to do is tell that someone where he is, and they'll do the rest."

For a moment they were all silent. Then Ron burst out laughing. "Oh, that's great!" he managed to gasp out between peals of laughter. "Just find out who he is. Just like that. *Who are you, little boy?* Of course, he doesn't speak English, and we don't speak Arabic, but don't let that stop us. If Jenny says it will work, it will work!"

Jenny waited for the laughter to die down. Then she observed calmly that she hadn't told them her plan yet.

This set Ron off again, and again Jenny waited until he and the others had stopped laughing.

"Just because we can't read or understand Arabic, it doesn't mean that he can't *write* it. If he were to write something, all we'd have to do would be to take it to Mr. Pritchard, and he could tell us what it means."

Again they were silent, but this time it was a respectful silence. Even Ron looked interested. "How are you going to get him to write anything?"

Jenny turned to Lauren who had had the midafternoon shift. "When the men take the boy down to the beach, they usually stand on the high part of the beach, don't they?"

Lauren nodded. "I think so. At least, that's where they've stood the times that I've seen them."

"That's where I've seen them stand, too," Ty agreed.

"Does the boy face them when he's playing, or does he face toward the ocean?"

"He's usually facing the ocean."

Jenny stared down at the sand, thinking. Finally she turned to Billy. "Billy, if you were that boy, and when you went to the beach, you found a sand castle with nobody near it, you'd go over and look at it, wouldn't you?"

Billy agreed that he would.

"If you found a sharpened pencil and a piece of paper lying in the center of the castle, would it give you any ideas?"

Billy looked puzzled. "What do you mean?"

"Those men are holding you against your will, and you want to get away. You find pencil and paper lying in the sand castle. Wouldn't it give you the idea of writing a message?"

"The men would see him if he tried to write a message," Ron objected.

"How would they see him? He has his back to them."

"What makes you think he'd catch on?" Billy asked cautiously.

"I think he's smart. Besides, why would there be a pencil and a piece of paper left in a sand castle unless someone had left them there on purpose?"

"How would he know they had been left for him?" Ty asked.

"Why else would anyone leave them?"

"I can think of lots of reasons."

"Let's hear them."

"Well . . ." Ty looked down at his feet. Then he looked up with a sheepish grin. "I guess I can't think of that many."

"If I were that boy," Jenny continued, "I wouldn't

care *who* found my message, so long as it wasn't one of the two men. Asking for help is better than doing nothing."

"But no one would understand his message," Billy objected.

"Maybe no one would, but then again maybe someone would find it who could understand it. Either that, or they would take it to someone who could. After all, why would they have left the paper and pencil?"

They talked a while longer, but no one could come up with another plan that seemed half as good as Jenny's, and they finally decided to give it a try. Then Ron asked how they could be sure the boy and the men would be coming to the beach on the day they built the sand castle.

"We can't be sure. We'll just have to build a sand castle each sunny day and wait."

"What if one of the men finds the paper and pencil?" Billy asked. "Won't that warn them?"

"Maybe, but why should they find it? Lauren just said they usually stand on the upper part of the beach. It seems to me we have to take that chance."

"When do you want to build the castle?" Ty asked.

"Tomorrow. Let's meet here after breakfast."

"What if it rains?"

"We'll wait a day."

"Do you really think it will work?"

Jenny turned to Ron. "It will work," she said firmly. "Like I said, the boy's smart."

15 The Sand Castle

R ARELY had Jenny awaited a new day as eagerly as
she did the day after the meeting, but when she
awakened, it was to the steady drumming of rain on
the roof, and the rain continued through the rest of the
day. Although she went out once or twice, it was obvious that no one would be on the beach, and she knew
that they would have to wait a day. Part of the morning she read. Then she tried to teach Finder to fetch
her slippers. He got the idea quickly, but he seemed to
take delight in bringing anything and everything but
the slippers. Ron and Lauren, who had come over late
in the morning, thought it was very funny, but Jenny
was far too irritated to appreciate the humor. She was

still out of sorts when they played Monopoly that afternoon, and even the pleasure of winning did not entirely soothe her. If Finder wondered why his supper was later than usual, he had only his own doggy sense of humor to blame for it.

Next day there was a pea-soup fog in the early morning, and Jenny thought that they would have to put off their plan again, but shortly after ten o'clock the fog burned off, and by ten-thirty the sun was shining brightly. They had decided the afternoon before that Jenny and Lauren would build the sand castle at around one o'clock. Then Ron would start fishing fifty yards east of where they expected the boy to come out. Jenny had cautioned him to stay far enough away so that the men would not be disturbed by his presence, but near enough so that he would be able to see what the boy did. As an added precaution, she had assigned Billy to watch from their old observation post in the dunes.

At twelve-thirty the four of them started up the beach toward Mariners Haven. Ty and Win had wanted to go, too, but Jenny had assigned them the task of keeping the dogs. She and Lauren intended to go back as soon as the sand castle was built, leaving Ron and Billy to do the watching. The boys had sandwiches, and they had told their families they were going fishing, and not to expect them back until late in the afternoon.

As they walked up the beach, Jenny was relieved to see that the tide was still going out. This was important because she didn't want their sand castle to be overrun by the incoming tide, nor did she want to build it so far up the beach that the men would be tempted to take a closer look. For some time they walked in silence. Then Ron asked what he should do if the castle got knocked down, or if the paper and pencil were taken from it by some passerby. Jenny had brought an extra pencil and piece of paper, and she handed them to Ron. He stuffed them in his trouser pocket, repeating his question about what he should do if the castle were to be knocked down.

"It depends on the time. Do you have a watch?"

Ron nodded, holding up his arm so that she could see the watch on his wrist.

"They usually come down to the beach around two o'clock, don't they?"

Again Ron nodded.

"If it's more than half an hour before two, you can fix it up again. If it's later than that, leave it, and we can build another one tomorrow."

"What if it gets knocked down and the men see the paper and pencil?" Billy asked.

"Ron can pick them up before they see them."

"I'll have to get close to do that."

"So get close!" Lauren glanced at Ron impatiently and turned to Jenny. "What will we do after we build the castle?"

"Go back to Mid Station."

"Think we could watch?"

Jenny hesitated. "We told Ty and Win we'd be coming back."

"They won't mind. We can watch from the dunes. Then when it's over, we'll all meet on the beach." She turned to Ron. "Okay?"

Ron glanced at Billy and nodded. "Okay. I'll go back along the beach, and Billy can take the path through the Holly Grove."

They had reached the path from the gray house now, and Billy and the girls dropped to the sand to build the castle, while Ron watched them, his fishing rod propped against his shoulder. Jenny had always liked building sand castles, which was one reason she had thought of her plan in the first place. She set to work now, scooping out the sand from what would be the moat and shaping it into a broad, rounded outer wall. Billy and Lauren had started from the other side, and their sections of the wall gradually closed the circle to meet her own.

"Wouldn't it be easier to start from the middle and work out?" Ron asked.

He was right, of course, but none of them was about to admit it.

"We're building the castle," Lauren observed tartly, "and we'll build it the way we want to."

"Okay. If you want to make it harder for yourselves, go ahead."

"It happens to be easier to build it this way. If we were to start from the middle, we might not make it big enough."

Ron laughed outright at this, and the others went on with their work, ignoring him. They had completed the outer wall and were building an inner wall, which was both higher and thicker. Lauren had brought an empty bottle with her, and she ran down to the surf periodically to fill it with water, which they used to dampen the sand. They made two tunnels, one on either side of the inner wall, and they put towers above the tunnels. When they were satisfied with the inner wall, they climbed into the trench between the two walls and began to work on the interior of the castle, building yet another wall through which there were several tunnels with a network of roads leading off from them. In the very center of the castle they built a high, thick wall around a central square. It was here that Jenny placed the paper and pencil.

"Are you sure he'll be able to see it?" Billy asked.

"He'll see it. If he comes to look at the castle, he'll be standing right over it."

Billy stood up. "I sure hope he gets the idea."

"He'll get it. He's sharp."

Jenny glanced at Lauren, who nodded agreement. The four of them stood for some time, looking out over the water and talking about their impressions of the boy. Then Ron glanced at his watch and told them it was almost one-thirty. Taking the hint, Jenny went over the plan one final time. Then she and Lauren wished the boys luck and started down the beach toward Mid Station. Halfway there they turned away from the water and scrambled over the front dune. Finding a secure spot, they settled to watch.

Ron had started to fish and was moving along the surf in the direction they had taken, while Billy was no longer in sight. Jenny looked toward where he would be watching, then back at Ron. It would be strange if he caught anything, but the surf was like that. Often when conditions were just right, you caught nothing; whereas on a day when everything seemed wrong, the fish would come in. She turned her eyes back to the dune line. If the boy was coming to the beach, he should appear at any moment. She watched, and suddenly the boy and the two men stepped into view.

The boy was wearing a bathing suit as usual, but he was also carrying a towel. Jenny was surprised by this. The boy had never brought a towel to the beach before, and it made her wonder if the men would allow him to swim. She noticed that niether one of them was wearing a bathing suit; would they have to go in with all their clothes on if the boy got into trouble? And what if he refused to swim in to shore? Jenny watched them cross the beach, and abruptly she was struck by another possibility. If the boy ran directly down to the water and waded in, the men would probably come to the front part of the beach to watch him. Wouldn't they be likely to see the paper and pencil hidden in the sand castle?

Jenny glanced toward where Ron was fishing, and her eye was caught by a movement in the water. A tail appeared in the center of a large swirl, and there were two other swirls off to one side. Evidently Ron had seen them at the same time she did, because he reeled in his line and ran along the beach to where the fish were swirling. As he cast out, the men and the boy noticed him for the first time. A fish jumped all the way out of the water, and the boy pointed excitedly. Apparently the men, too, were intrigued, because they moved in Ron's direction, walking a few paces behind the boy. Once the boy started to dash ahead, but he stopped abruptly, looking back at the two men. Jenny guessed that he had been told not to run ahead.

Ron was waiting, ready to cast as soon as the fish showed. His earlier casts had been fruitless, and he had evidently decided to wait until he had a target. Suddenly a fish broke beyond the third wave and to his right. Ron cast instantly, dropping the plug just inshore of the fish. He jerked it once, then again, and the fish hit, knocking the plug into the air. Ron continued the retrieve, and two jerks later he got a second strike. This time the fish was on, and Ron's rod bent in a tight arc. The boy called out, gesturing to the two men, who quickly joined him. Evidently it was a good fish, and Jenny could tell from the way Ron was holding the rod that the fish was stripping line from the reel. Then Ron began to work the fish, and it moved down the beach to Ron's left. He glanced over his shoulder, and even as he did so, his rod straightened and the line went slack. Ron reeled in slowly, looked at his plug, and cast out again. The fish had gotten off.

The boy and the two men watched a short while longer. Then the bald man called to the boy, and the three of them walked back to their usual spot. The boy saw the sand castle and headed directly toward it, but the men remained where they were, evidently deep in conversation. Then they strolled to the upper part of the beach, sitting down on the towel that the boy had brought. Jenny strained her eyes to see what the boy was doing, but he was squatting with his back to her, and she could see nothing.

"Do you think he found the note?" she whispered to Lauren.

"He must have."

The boy continued to play by the sand castle for some time. The bald man was sitting with his chin on his knees, and the other man had stretched out on his back. It appeared to Jenny that the bald man was watching Ron fish, although now and again he would glance toward the boy. Finally the boy got to his feet and ran toward the edge of the surf. As he reached the water, he turned in response to a call from the man and shouted something back. Then he waded in. Watching him, it seemed to Jenny that he was slowly working his way toward Ron, but before she could be sure of this, Ron's rod suddenly bent again. He had switched to a bottom lure, and a fish had taken it out near the end of his cast.

Immediately the boy splashed to shore and ran down the beach until he was standing only ten yards or so from Ron. The bald man, too, had jumped up, and he quickly joined the boy, and the two of them stood together, watching Ron fight the fish. The second man remained where he was and watched from a distance. Apparently the fish was smaller than the first, and Ron was able to control the fight from the beginning. He soon had the fish near the shore, and seconds later he was sliding it up on the sand. It was a bluefish of two or three pounds. Removing the hooks from its mouth, Ron tossed it well up the beach and cast again.

As he was casting, Jenny saw the boy say something to the man. The man hesitated, then nodded, and the boy ran forward and squatted down next to the fish. The man started to follow him, but changed his mind and called to the boy instead. The boy jumped up immediately and returned to where the man was standing, but in those few seconds when he had been squatting next to the fish, Jenny thought that she had seen him slip something under the fish. Lauren agreed. The two girls watched tensely, afraid that the man would change his mind and walk over to look at the fish, but he didn't. He and the boy returned to where the other man was sitting on the towel. A few minutes later they left the beach.

As soon as they were out of sight, Jenny and Lauren scrambed down to the beach and started toward where Ron was still fishing. On the way Billy joined them. He, too, had seen the boy pull something out of his bathing suit and was afraid that Ron would miss it. When Ron saw them coming, he reeled in his line and walked to meet them.

"Are they back in the house?" he asekd.

Billy nodded. "They hung up the towel to dry and went right in."

"That was crazy the way it happened." Ron stared out over the water, shaking his head. "Who would have figured bluefish would come in the middle of the day at low tide? I guess I kind of messed things up."

"What do you mean you messed things up?"

"I was supposed to be watching, and I was so busy fishing I forgot to watch."

"You did all right," Jenny assured him. "Were you watching when the boy went over to the sand castle?"

"Yes, but I didn't see much. I thought he might have been writing something, but I couldn't tell for sure. I got a strike just about then, and when I looked back later, he was just fooling around in the sand."

"I think he did write something," Jenny said quietly, "and I'll bet we find it under the fish you caught."

She walked over quickly and pushed the fish aside with her foot. Under it was a piece of paper, which had been rolled up and stuck through a ring. She looked at the ring carefully. It was gold, she guessed, almost like a wedding band, and there was a design running all the way around it. Passing it to Lauren, she unfolded the note. It was brief, and the writing was like the writing they had seen on the newspaper. Refolding it, she slipped it into her pocket with the ring, which Lauren had returned to her.

"How did you know the message was here?" Ron asked.

"We saw him put it here. You were fishing, so you didn't notice."

Jenny turned and started up the beach toward where they had built the sand castle.

"What are you doing?" Lauren called after her.

"I want to be sure he didn't leave the pencil in the sand castle."

It wasn't there. Jenny guessed that the boy had thrown it away or buried it. Retracing her steps, she joined the others, and they set off toward Mid Station. On the way back they talked over what had happened and speculated on the size of the fish that Ron had lost. Ron was sure it had been a bluefish. He had had one quick look at it, and his guess was that it would have gone at least eight or nine pounds. He thought he had lost it because his drag had been too tight, and Jenny agreed. As they approached Mid Station, the twins ran to meet them with Rex and Finder at their heels.

"What happened?" Win called breathlessly as soon as she was in shouting distance.

Reaching in her pocket, Jenny extracted the ring and the message and held them up. "The plan worked!" she called back. "We've got a message!"

"Tell us what happened," Win pleaded anxiously. "Tell us everything."

Jenny obliged, describing all that had occurred, and passing the note and the ring for the twins to examine. Then she suggested they go to Mr. Pritchard's house to get the note translated.

Mr. Pritchard was sitting on the front porch with Mr. Pruett and Mr. Ketchum. *Maybe we'd better come back later,* Billy whispered to Jenny when he saw them, but Jenny shook her head. Besides, Mr. Pritchard had already seen them. "By golly, now there's a sight to gladden an ancient pair of eyes," he said cheerfully. "It's the younger generation coming in force." Winking broadly at Mr. Pruett and Mr. Ketchum, he turned to Jenny. "Well, young lady, what can I do for you?"

"We have something we want you to read for us."

"Read for you?" Mr. Pritchard looked at her shrewdly, his eyes passing from her to Billy, and on to the rest. "It couldn't be by any chance that you've been snooping around that house in Mariners Haven again, could it?"

"We have a message from the boy."

"You do?" Mr. Pritchard was alert now. He glanced quickly at Mr. Ketchum and Mr. Pruett before turning again to Jenny. "How did you get it?"

Jenny quickly explained all that they had done since they had last talked to him. Mr. Pritchard listened closely, his eyes beginning to twinkle more and more. After she had finished, he was silent for some time. Then he spoke, and they could tell that he was excited.

"Well, this should clinch it. You kids have done a good job, and I think you're going to be in for quite a surprise before long."

"What kind of surprise?" Jenny asked quickly.

"Let me see the note. I don't want to go leaping to conclusions."

Jenny handed him the note and the ring through which it had been stuck. Mr. Pritchard put on his glasses and read the note. Then he looked at the ring, turning it back and forth in his hand.

"What does the note say, Mr. Pritchard?" Ty asked impatiently.

"It gives the boy's name and tells us whom to contact. I might add that I'm already in contact with the person he names."

"Who is he? I mean, the boy?"

Mr. Pritchard looked at Ty thoughtfully. Then he

turned away with a shake of his head. "I'd rather not answer that for now. I expect you'll find out soon enough. After reading that Cairo newspaper, I did a little nosing around as I told you I would. I think I'll have the contents of this note in the right hands by supper tonight, and I doubt you'll have to wait long to see some action."

"Won't you tell us anything?" Win asked plaintively.

"Not a thing. You'll just have to be patient. *And don't go near the gray house for the next couple of days!*" He looked at Jenny directly. "Do you understand? I don't want to alert those men. It's important."

"We won't."

Mr. Pritchard watched them. Then he turned to Mr. Ketchum and Mr. Pruett. "It's strange the way things happen in this world," he said. "An affair of governments can come down to a group of kids playing on the beach in summer. Odd, isn't it?"

"Not so odd," Mr. Pruett said with a smile. *"There is a divinity that shapes our ends, rough hew them how we will."*

"Shakespeare?" Billy asked.

Mr. Pruett cleared his throat, winking at Mr. Pritchard.

"Of course."

16 Confession

THE next two days seemed endless. Honoring their promise to Mr. Pritchard, Jenny and the others kept away from Mariners Haven, although they did watch the beach in front of the gray house from a distance. There was a definite reason for this, and the watching was done at Mr. Pritchard's request. He wanted to be sure there was no change in the daily routine of the boy and the two men. It seemed awful to Jenny that they couldn't find some way to let the boy know that his message had been received, but she knew Mr. Pritchard was right. They could not afford to take chances. They had done their share, and now it was up to the boy's friends to take the next step. Of course they tried to get Mr. Pritchard to tell them more, but they couldn't get a word out of him.

While she was waiting for something to happen, Jenny had a great deal to think about. Now that it appeared that the boy would be rescued, she could no longer avoid making a decision about Finder. Although she had told Lauren she was going to keep Finder, her conscience rebelled. After all, the boy probably loved Finder as much as she did, and it hardly seemed fair to take his pet away from him without giving him any choice in the matter. Like it or not, Finder belonged to him, and he should have the choice. To use his gratefulness to pry Finder from him seemed wrong, and try as she would, Jenny could not escape her awareness of this. And yet, she wanted Finder. It was a dilemma, and as far as she could see, there was no way out. Besides, even if the boy should decide to give Finder to her, there was still the problem of where Finder would spend the coming winter. Nothing had been said since Mr. Martin had suggested he stay with the Sargeants, but Jenny knew her father, and she doubted that he would change his mind. Just thinking about it made her mad, but there was nothing she could do.

She was worried, too, about how her parents would react when they discovered what she had done. Mr. Martin had told her to stay away from the gray house in Mariners Haven, and she had disobeyed him. Sooner or later it would come out, and Jenny guessed that it would be better if she were to speak first. The question was *when?* Billy urged her to wait, arguing that once it all came out about the boy and how they had helped him, the Martins would have to forgive her, but Jenny didn't agree. She felt that it would be cowardly to wait, and that her parents would like it far better if she were to speak up now. In fact, talking with Billy convinced her that she could not afford to wait, and she decided to tell them that night at supper.

Mr. and Mrs. Martin had gone to the mainland for the day, and they did not return until late. They had spent four days away from the beach during the past week. Twice they had played golf, and the other two times they had gone on business. When they returned, they were hot and tired, and Jenny was tempted to put off her confession until the next morning, but a glance at Billy squirming uneasily in his chair decided her that she had better get it over with. Mrs. Martin had cooked hamburgers and peas mixed with rice for supper, and their plates were almost empty when Jenny judged that the time was right.

"I have something to tell you," she said abruptly, turning to her father.

Mr. Martin looked up from his plate, his eyes resting briefly on Jenny, and then swinging to his wife. "That sounds ominous, doesn't it, Betty?"

"I disobeyed you."

"You did?" Mr. Martin's eyes were again on Jenny, and he was watching her closely.

"I didn't stay away from the gray house in Mariners Haven. I did some other things, too."

Mr. Martin took a final bite of his supper. Then he wiped his mouth and pushed his chair back from the table. "Want to tell us about it?"

Jenny told all that had happened, leaving nothing out. It made a long story, and the Martins asked several questions in the course of it. When Jenny told about her visit to the gray house, they both frowned, their expressions grim. By the time she had finished, although their expressions were still somber, there was something in their manner that made her a wee bit hopeful, but she didn't let it show.

"All right, let's consider this," Mr. Martin said finally. "In the first place, I'm glad you decided to tell me. Mr. Pritchard told me a few things yesterday afternoon, and I was hoping you would speak up. That's a strong plus.

"Naturally I'm not happy about your disobedience. In fact, I'm very unhappy about it." He looked up quickly. "I hope you realize that when we tell you and Billy not to do something, we have our reasons. You yourselves could have been hurt, and the other children who were with you as well. What you were doing was dangerous, and furthermore, you were trespassing on someone else's property. It may have turned out for the best, but that has nothing to do with it. It could just as easily have turned out badly."

Jenny nodded miserably. She could not meet her father's eyes, nor could she look away. She scrunched down in her chair, waiting for the axe to fall.

"So here we are," Mr. Martin resumed. "As it happens, everything has turned out well, and if that little boy is rescued, and we hope he will be, he'll have you to thank for his freedom. That's the silver lining. The fact remains you two chose to put yourselves and your friends in very real danger against our express orders, and you, Jen, went so far out of line that you were guilty of the crime of breaking and entering. What the dickens got into you?"

Jenny did not even try to answer. There was nothing to be said. Mr. Martin watched her for a moment.

"One thing I'm curious about, Jen. I wonder if you thought that your mother and I would be willing to let the whole thing slide because it turned out well."

"No," was Jenny's barely audible response. She wanted to say more, but the dryness of her throat and mouth made it impossible.

"I'm glad of that. Well, like it or not, it's done. The question is what are we going to do about it? It would be easy enough to punish the two of you. That's what I thought I'd do at first, but as your mother and I have talked about it, I've changed my mind. You punish someone for lying, or cheating, or not doing something they were supposed to do, but this is far too serious for that. This cannot be allowed to happen again, *ever!*"

He stared at them, and reluctantly each in turn met his glance.

"All right. Now you two had better get to bed. I think the boy's friends will be coming tomorrow from what Mr. Pritchard told me, and you'll want to have had a good night's sleep."

"Can we go with them when they rescue the boy?" Billy asked.

"Absolutely not! This was no business for children

from the beginning, and it certainly isn't now."

Jenny walked to the door and let Finder in. Then she said good night to her parents and stepped into her room. She was relieved, and she was looking forward to tomorrow, but she was worried, too. Tomorrow she would have to make a decision, and she still didn't know what she was going to do.

17 Prince Abou

Jenny woke up early the next morning. Her father and mother were still sleeping, but Billy was awake, and the two of them slipped into their clothes and stepped quietly out onto the deck where they could talk. Finder went out with them and started to hunt immediately, running through the back yard and into the tall beach grass behind the Rollins house. As soon as they were both seated, Jenny observed that it was lucky she had decided to speak out. Billy agreed.

"It wouldn't have been so bad if you hadn't gone into the house," he added. "That's the thing that really ticked Dad off."

"I suppose it was stupid," Jenny admitted, "but it

just sort of happened, and it seemed like a good idea at the time."

"Maybe, but Dad's right. You could have gotten into a lot of trouble."

Jenny was watching the birds on the feeder as they talked. There were two towhees picking at the remnants of yesterday's feeding. She had learned to recognize them by their call, which sounded exactly like their name: toe—ee. As she watched, a female cardinal flew across the bushes in quick, darting swoops, landing on the rim of the tray, her olive-green cap riding jauntily above her small, bright eyes and blunt, orange-yellow beak. The towhees flew down to the sand as she arrived, leaving the feeding tray to her, but she had to give way in turn when a bluejay arrived in a fluff of feathers. Jenny stood up quickly, waving her arms, and the bluejay flew away.

"Why did you do that?" Billy asked.

"I don't like bluejays. They're bullies."

"I like them. They're not scared of anything."

"Who says they're not scared. Bullies usually are scared."

"Bluejays don't bully other birds just because they want to be bullies," Billy objected. "They're competing for food. It's like the men who are guarding the boy. Their job is to watch him. One of the men is nice to him, but the bald-headed one is nasty. He's a bully, and the other man isn't."

"Do you think they'd hurt the boy if they thought he was going to be rescued?"

"I don't know. Maybe."

Jenny looked at Billy. She hadn't considered this, and it frightened her.

"I think I'll get some bird food," she said finally.

Getting to her feet, Jenny slipped back into the house. To her surprise both her parents were up, and the coffee was brewing on the stove.

"You two on the deck?" Mr. Martin inquired when he saw her. Jenny nodded, and he asked if they would like some coffee-milk.

"Yes, please."

"I'll bring it out. Tell Billy I'll bring him some, too."

"I will."

Taking the bag of birdseed and a funnel from their place on the shelf, she ran quickly out to the feeder, noting with satisfaction that the bluejay was nowhere in sight. Inserting the narrow point of the funnel into the hole on top of the feeder, she poured a steady stream of seeds until the glass compartment was three-quarters full. Then she replaced the cork stopper and returned to the deck, leaving the funnel and the bag of birdseed near the kitchen door.

"Mommy and Daddy are up," she announced as she sat down in her former spot. "Daddy's making coffee-milk for us."

"Is he in a good mood?"

"I think so. Why?"

"I was just wondering."

"Anyone for coffee-milk?"

Turning, they saw their mother standing by the back door with two steaming cups, and they hurried across the deck to take them from her. Mr. Martin followed, carrying two additional cups, and they all sat down to drink their coffee. Mr. Martin was the first to speak.

"You know, there's one thing I didn't say last night. We've talked over the disobedience part of it, and I think we understand each other, but there's another side to it. Even if what you did was mistaken in some respects, the fact remains that you both acted with considerable wisdom overall and with a good deal of courage. The idea of watching the house to learn their routine and the scheme you devised to give the boy a chance to write a message were very sharp. Mr. Pritchard couldn't get over it, and I must say your mother and I are very proud of you. I don't mean to take away from anything I said last night, but I like to give credit where credit's due."

"Did you talk to Mr. Pritchard last night?" Jenny asked.

"Yes. He came over after you went to bed. Which reminds me. We'd better get going. I have a feeling today is going to be a very busy day."

Half an hour later as they were finishing breakfast, there was a knock on the front door. Jenny hurried to open it and returned, followed by Mr. Pritchard and five other men whom she had never seen before. It was Mr. Pritchard who performed the introductions.

"This is Mr. and Mrs. Martin and their children, Jenny and Billy. The gentleman at my right is Prince Abou Sufyan, who is the envoy to the United Nations of the sheikdom of Hejaz. Behind him are four gentlemen of his staff: Omar Ben Kilabeh, Ibrahim El

Mehdi, Haroun Ben Zaideh, and Ghanim Ben Bekkar. Abou, perhaps you can explain our business to the Martins."

"With pleasure."

The tall, heavyset man at Mr. Pritchard's side stepped forward. He was smiling, and his eyes seemed to twinkle behind the thick-lensed, black-rimmed glasses he wore. He looked directly at Jenny and Billy, and his smile broadened.

"I suppose with the intelligence you've already shown, you two have long since guessed why we are here. My old friend Pritchard tells me that you've been very put out with him, because he wouldn't tell you all you wanted to know. Well, I hope I can satisfy your curiosity, and in return, I think you can help us. What would you like to know?"

Before Jenny or Billy could answer, Mrs. Martin interrupted to suggest that they all sit outside on the deck, and she asked the Prince and his staff whether they would like coffee. The Prince thanked her and said they would, and while she went into the kitchen to get the coffee, Mr. Martin led the way to the back deck. When they were settled, Prince Abou repeated his question.

"Is the boy your son?" Jenny asked quickly.

Prince Abou smiled. "No, but I almost feel as if he were. Prince Shikry Abou Homad is my nephew. His father, my brother, is our Sheik or King. Prince Shikry was kidnapped the first week in June in New York City where he was staying with me at the request of his father, so you can imagine how I've felt during the last two months. Fortunately Mr. Pritchard and I have been friends for many years. When he told me what you had told him about seeing the boy, I was sure it was Prince Shikry. You can imagine how surprised Mr. Pritchard was when I told him. Naturally he had no idea of the kidnapping."

"Do the police know about it?" Mr. Martin enquired.

"No, the matter was too delicate to allow us to call in the police. Unfortunately, once something becomes official, it is difficult to keep secret. In this particular case, we could not afford to have it known that Prince Shikry had disappeared."

Prince Abou paused to sip the coffee that Mrs. Martin had handed to him. Then he set the cup on the table beside him.

"Let me explain the situation to you. There was an attack on my brother, the Sheik, last March, and he was fatally wounded. He has been lingering between life and death for the past five months, and there is little hope that he will recover. Nonetheless, he was conscious for a day or so after the attack before he fell into a coma, and one of his first instructions was that Prince Shikry should be flown immediately to New York to stay with me. The reason for this is that Prince Shikry is the heir to the throne, and he was afraid that those who had tried to kill him might harm the Prince. As you can see, he was only too correct."

"Why haven't they . . ."

"Killed him?" Prince Abou leaned back in his chair. "The reason for that has to do with the laws of our country. When the Sheik dies, a new Sheik must be crowned within twenty-four hours. It is an old tradition that has become law. There must be no day in the history of Hejaz without a ruler seated on the throne. We believe now that my middle brother was behind the attack on the Sheik. Since he is older than I am, he would be next in line were it not for Prince Shikry. I think he intended to remove Shikry long enough so that he would be crowned in his place. Then, since he is childless, I imagine he would have adopted Shikry as his heir. I don't want to burden you with politics, but my brother hates everything that the Sheik and I stand for. If he were to become Sheik, I would be banished, and Hejaz would become a harsh and cruel land."

"I still don't understand why you didn't tell the police or F.B.I.," Mr. Martin said.

"We told both the F.B.I. and the C.I.A., and they have been helping us. You see, this is our problem. I'm sure my brother would prefer to keep Prince Shikry alive, but I have no doubt that his guards have been instructed to kill him rather than surrender him. My brother wants the throne, and if he has to kill Prince Shikry to get it, he will kill him. That is why we cannot afford to alarm Shikry's guards until we are in a position to protect Shikry from them, and that is why we are here this morning. Do you have any other questions?"

"I have one," Mrs. Martin said, speaking for the first time. "Why did they bring your nephew to Fire Island? I would have thought that they would have hidden him far away from here, or even taken him back to Hejaz."

"Your question is a good one," Prince Abou admitted. "I think they felt that it was too dangerous to try to carry Shikry back to Hejaz. Besides, they didn't want to frighten the boy. Remember that my brother hopes to take over his education and name him his heir. I believe they chose Fire Island for two reasons. The first is that this island is very similar to Kair Bin Said where Shikry was raised. It has the added advantage of being a community where many people rent their houses, and strangers are less likely to be noticed. Secondly, I expect the house seemed an ideal hiding place, because it belongs to a man with whom Shikry's father and I have done a great deal of business and whom we trusted. His house would be the last place in the world we would look for Shikry. Furthermore, it is isolated, and yet is close to New York City and JFK airport. I think it was an excellent choice, and we are lucky through your children's efforts to have found Shikry. We owe them many thanks."

"Don't thank us," Billy objected, pointing to Finder. "Thank Finder."

"Pritchard told me about your little dog," Prince Abou said, smiling down at Finder. "That was a stroke of luck, too. Shikry and I were out walking one day, and he saw this dog in a pet store window. Of course, I told him he could have any dog he chose, but he wasn't interested in any of the others. He wanted this dog. The men guarding Shikry made a bad mistake when they tried to chase the dog away."

"May I ask you about that?" Jenny asked quickly.

"About what, young lady?"

"Why do you think they drove Finder away? If they hadn't done that, we never would have known a thing."

"Well, when they kidnapped Shikry, he was walking the dog. They disposed of his bodyguard and took the boy and the dog off in a car, bringing him directly to Fire Island. Probably, once they were here, they decided that the dog would be a nuisance and chased it away, assuming that it would find a new home, as it eventually did."

"But then they tied Finder up," Jenny pointed out. "He was gone for three days, and when he came back, he had a rope around his neck. Mr. Ketchum said that he had seen him tied to a post at the gray house."

"I didn't know that." Prince Abou glanced at Mr. Pritchard before turning again to Jenny. "It does seem strange," he admitted, "but perhaps when the dog turned up again, they decided to take it back to the mainland. Either that, or they may have regretted their first decision to drive the dog away. Don't forget that they're under orders to frighten the boy as little as possible. I'm sure he's been fed a pack of lies to explain why he's being kept here."

"Why are they so rough with him then?"

"They're probably less rough than it seems to you. Prince Shikry has grown up with bodyguards. Unfortunately, men who live with violence are not accustomed to showing gentleness. I doubt that he has found these men very different from those he has known before. Now, if you've finished with your questions, it's time for action. Pritchard tells me that you've been keeping some kind of schedule of what Shikry's captors do every day. Could I see it?"

Jenny had brought the chart from Lauren's house the day before and went to her room to get it. Returning, she handed it to Prince Abou, who studied it carefully before passing it to the men of his staff. He waited until they had looked it over. Then he turned to the man who had been introduced as Ghanim Ben Bekkar.

"I think the time when they are on the beach offers the best opportunity. What do you think, Ghanim?"

Rather than answering the Prince, Ghanim turned to Jenny. He spoke with a thick accent, but she had no trouble understanding him. "When they are on the beach, is it that they stand in a group, or are they, how you say, divided?"

"Usually they come out in a group, and then the boy goes down to play near the surf, while the men stay on the high part of the beach and watch him."

Ghanim turned to the Prince. "Perhaps we shoot from behind the dunes . . ."

Prince Abou shook his head. "Let us avoid bloodshed." He turned to Mr. Pritchard. "Would it be possible to obtain one of those cars that drive along the beach?"

Mr. Pritchard nodded.

"If we were to drive between Shikry and the men, we could rescue the boy and capture them."

"Would they allow us to drive between them and Prince Shikry?" Ghanim asked. "There would be danger, your Highness."

"You could use a police car," Jenny suggested. "I saw a police car drive between the boy and the men twice four days ago. The police drive down the beach really fast when there's an emergency."

Prince Abou stared at Jenny for a moment. Then he turned to Mrs. Martin with a smile. "Your children are a fountain of inspiration."

"Sometimes," was her rejoinder, although she smiled at Jenny proudly.

"What do you think, Ghanim?" Prince Abou asked.

"The girl's plan is good," Ghanim affirmed. "There is still danger, but it is less. Only ambush is safe." Again he turned to Jenny. "The men, little Miss, do they know anything? Are they . . ." He searched for the word he wanted. "Are they suspecting?"

"I don't think so."

"Good." Prince Abou rose from his chair, and the others rose with him. He shook hands with Mr. and Mrs. Martin. Then he stepped across to Jenny and Billy. "Our country owes you a great debt," he announced solemnly. "If we are successful today, I hope Prince Shikry will be able to thank you in person before nightfall, Allah willing. For now, I thank you on his behalf, and I hope you'll each accept these small tokens of our gratitude."

With that he made a sign to one of his staff, and the man stepped forward with two small boxes, handing one to each of them. Jenny opened hers quickly, and she was dazzled by the contents. Set in royal blue velvet was a ring almost exactly like the one through which the boy had stuck his message, but instead of a design circling the band, it was circled by gleaming, clear-white stones, which she learned later were diamonds, and in the center was a brilliant green stone in the shape of a tiny heart. Billy's ring was almost identical, except that his green stone was cut in the shape of an egg.

"They're beautiful," Jenny whispered finally, looking at her mother for reassurance, "but we weren't the only ones. There were Lauren, and Ron, and the twins."

"Don't worry," Prince Abou assured her. "I have something for each of them as well, but that will come later. It's getting late, and we'd best be off to make our arrangements."

Picking up the chart, he thanked the Martins for their hospitality, and he and his staff and Mr. Pritchard started for the door. Long after they had gone, Jenny continued to stare at the ring. It was so beautiful when she put it on her finger that she could hardly believe it. Billy said that it made her look like a princess, and she secretly agreed. Finally she and Billy handed the rings to their father for safekeeping and started for the kitchen door. Jenny was about to step inside, when Finder bounded up the steps and darted in front of her.

"Finder!" she exclaimed, and suddenly she stopped dead. This was it. This was the day of reckoning. By suppertime Finder might no longer be hers. She stood motionless, staring down at him. Then she picked him up and took him to her bed, where she buried her head against his warm side. She was still lying there silently, when her mother stepped into the room and sat down on the bed next to her.

"It's hard, isn't it?" she said softly.

Jenny nodded.

"You know, Jen, generosity is something that people talk about a lot, but very few people practice. It's easy to give up things you don't really want, and that's as far as most people go. Real generosity is giving up something really important to you; something you want so badly you feel it in every part of you."

"Like I feel about Finder."

"The way you feel about Finder. If he belongs to Prince Shikry, you'll have a decision to make. If you're generous, and I know this won't be easy, you'll hide your hurt, and you'll make the boy feel that you're happy to be able to return his dog. That way you won't be clouding his happiness by making him feel that you're unhappy."

"It's sort of a test, isn't it?"

"In a way. It will only work if you really mean it. I wouldn't blame you a bit if you felt that was too much to ask. It will take a lot of thinking."

Jenny looked up at her mother. Then she looked away, but she didn't speak. Her mother sat on the bed a moment more, absently petting Finder. Then she left the room.

18 A Matter of Timing

JENNY remained in her room for almost an hour, thinking about what her mother had said. Then, her mind made up, she suggested to Billy that they go tell the others what had happened. They crossed quickly to the Rollins house, but Ron was not there, and they continued down to the bay. On the way Billy asked what Jenny intended to do, but she pretended not to hear him. When the reached the bay, they found Ron, Lauren, and the twins gathered around two small sailboats. Evidently they were planning to race them, but the race was quickly forgotten when they saw the two Martins and heard Jenny's shout that she had news. They rushed over, and Jenny quickly told them about Prince Shikry and how he had been kidnapped. Then she told about the gifts, which brought startled exclamations from all, especially when they heard that there would be something for each of them. Finally she told about the rescue plan.

"I'd sure like to watch," Ty muttered when she had finished.

"I would, too," Win agreed.

"We can, but we'd better not get anywhere close. It would mess everything up if the men saw us. Besides, there may be shooting, and someone could get hurt."

"Do you really think they might kill the men?" Lauren asked.

Jenny shook her head. "Probably not. Prince Abou says that he doesn't want bloodshed; but if the men put up a fight, I guess they will. Chances are they'll give up, though."

"I'll bet they don't," Ty disagreed. "I'll bet they fight it out." He fell into a gunfighter's crouch, pretending to draw a revolver and fire it. The others ignored him.

"Hey, I've got an idea," Ron suggested. "Why don't we watch what happens through binoculars? That way we can watch without getting anywhere close."

"What if the sun reflects off the binoculars?" Billy asked.

"It won't if we're careful. All we have to do is shade our glasses with cardboard so the sun doesn't hit the lens directly. What do you say?"

Ty stepped forward. "Let's!"

They all looked at Jenny, and after a moment, she

nodded. "Okay. We'll meet at Ty's and Win's house around one. That way we'll be ready when they come out on the beach."

The rest of the morning seemed to pass very slowly. Jenny spent most of it playing with Finder. Only when her mother announced that lunch was ready did she leave her pet, and she returned to him as soon as she had finished. Twenty minutes later Billy stepped out the back door, glasses in hand, and told her that it was time to go. Calling Finder, she joined him, and they hurried up the boardwalk toward the twins' house. The others were already there.

"Where are we going to watch from?" Lauren asked.

"Why don't we watch from the top of the dune over there?" Ron suggested, pointing to a high point to the west of the Parks house. "It's high enough so we can see, and there's plenty of cover."

"Okay, let's go."

Running quickly to the foot of the dune, they climbed to the top and nestled among the bushes. Lauren and Ron had their own glasses, and the twins and Billy and Jenny were each sharing a pair. The tide was all the way out and just starting to come in, and the sun was high in the sky. From where they were hiding they could see the beach in front of the gray house, and they watched eagerly for the first appearance of the boy and the two men.

"How will Prince Abou know when to drive up the beach?" Lauren asked.

"They have a lookout," Billy replied, pointing to a high point of land halfway between Mid Station and

Mariners Haven. Jenny took the glasses from Billy
and looked. She could see the man lying at the crest
of the dune with his back to them.

"He's got a rifle," Ty commented.

Jenny looked more closely and saw that Ty was
right. "That's probably just in case."

"I wish they'd come," Ty muttered impatiently.

"They'll come," Jenny assured him. She was holding Finder in her lap, while Rex lay at Ron's side,
panting heavily in the warm sunlight. Finder stirred
uneasily and looked up at her, and Jenny scratched
him behind the ears.

Suddenly Ron muttered tensely that they were coming and warned everyone to shade their glasses. They
all watched intently, passing the glasses back and forth.
The bald man was walking first, followed by the boy
and the other man. When they reached a point halfway between the dune line and the surf, they paused to
look out over the ocean. Jenny noticed with relief that
the boy was wearing his bathing suit and had a towel.
That meant that he would be down near the surf,
while the men remained on the high part of the
beach, watching him. The low tide meant that he
would be even further from them.

Training her glasses on the lookout, she could see
that he, too, had glasses and was looking through them.
She tried to guess which of the men he was, but she
could not see him clearly enough to be sure. Turning
her glasses back to the group on the beach, she was
just in time to see the boy start down to the surf, while
the men walked back up the beach a few yards and

seated themselves on the sand. She guessed that there was a space of roughly twenty-five yards between the men and the boy.

"Let me have the glasses," Billy whispered urgently.

Passing the glasses to him, Jenny kept her eyes on the boy. Without the glasses she would not have been able to recognize him, but she had no trouble following his movements even at the distance, although she could not see in any detail what he was doing. Fortunately it was a cool, clear day, and the heat haze was at a minimum, making for good visibility. She saw the boy hesitate at the edge of the surf, then wade into the water. Now was the time! She glanced quickly at the spot where the lookout was lying prone. Suddenly she saw him raise his arm as if signalling, and she turned to look toward Pirates Cove. Abruptly, as if by magic, two police cars pulled out of the cut and drove down to the flat part of the beach. Only when they reached the hard sand at the surf's edge and turned west did they put on their flashers and pick up speed, but they did not use their sirens. Evidently they did not want to alert the men guarding the boy any sooner than necessary. In no time, they had passed the spot where the children were watching. Jenny watched tensely. If only the boy stayed in the water and the men didn't move. . . .

The bald man had spotted the police cars now. He got to his feet, watching their approach. The boy was splashing happily in the surf, unaware of what was happening. The man cupped his hands to call something to the boy, but the boy obviously didn't hear him. The man started to walk forward, but the police cars were almost up to him, and he stopped, continuing to watch them. It was a matter of yards now, of feet . . . Then the police cars came to a skidding halt, and several men jumped out.

"They have guns," Billy whispered, his eyes glued to the glasses. "The men are putting up their hands! They've got them!"

"Let me see!" Jenny insisted, pulling the glasses away from Billy. Sure enough Prince Abou was holding the boy in his arms and whirling around and around. Jenny switched to the two men. They looked grim. The second car had been full of policemen, and one of them was slipping handcuffs on the bald man, while his companion stood glumly behind him, waiting his turn. Three of the men who had been with the Prince that morning were watching, and seconds later, the fourth came running up. He had been the lookout.

As soon as the handcuffs were on, the two men were hustled into the second police car, while the Prince and his staff and the boy climbed into the first. Then the cars turned and drove down the beach past them toward Pirates Cove.

"Do you think they'll come back here later?" Ty asked.

"I expect so," Jenny replied. "Let's go down to our house and wait."

Getting to her feet, she led the way back to the boardwalk with Finder trotting at her heels. For the others it was all over but the presents, but for her it had just begun.

19 Prince Abou Returns

W HEN the police car bearing Prince Abou Sufyan and the boy drove up to the Martin house, Mr. and Mrs. Martin stepped out to greet them, while Jenny and the others remained near the door. Mr. Pritchard was standing just behind Jenny. A policeman had driven Prince Abou to the house, and he remained in the car while the Prince and his nephew climbed out. As the boy stepped to the boardwalk, Finder, who had been standing next to Jenny, rushed forward and jumped against him, and the boy greeted him eagerly. In spite of herself, Jenny couldn't help but feel glad for the boy and Finder, but a pang of regret went through her. Meanwhile Prince Abou was being introduced to the other children, and he greeted each in turn solemnly and courteously. Then he turned to the boy who was standing next to him with Finder at his feet.

"As I think you all know by this time," Prince Abou began, "the boy whom you helped us to rescue is my nephew, Prince Shikry Abou Homad. He would like to thank each of you, and although he cannot speak your language, I know that you can imagine all he would like to say."

He smiled at the boy, who smiled back at him. Then, stepping up to Lauren, Prince Shikry spoke a few words, which they could not understand, after which he bowed. He did the same with each in turn, except that he shook hands with the boys instead of bowing. Finder had followed him on this round, and when he came to Jenny, Finder looked up at her eagerly, his tail wagging, as if to say: *I can't help it if I've met an old friend. It doesn't mean that I've forgotten you.* When the boy had spoken his brief speech and made his bow, Finder abruptly jumped up with his paws against Jenny's legs, looking over his shoulder at the boy. It was comical, and it made everybody laugh, but it took all Jenny's self-control to hold back her tears. She reached down to pet Finder, and then straightened, and as she did so, her eyes met those of the boy, and she saw in his eyes something very deep. He spoke in a soft voice, his eyes never leaving her face. Only when he had finished did he glance at his uncle, as if asking him to translate. Prince Abou hesitated, watching the boy. Finally he shrugged, and turned to Jenny to translate his nephew's words.

"Prince Shikry says that he can see that you and the dog are very close. He says that he, too, loves the dog; that it was a gift given to him by me when he first came to New York. He says that he would like you to have the dog to keep. He hopes that someday he will be able to return to see you and the dog again."

For a moment Jenny stood transfixed, not trusting herself to speak. It was what she had hoped against hope that he would say, and she was tempted as she had never been tempted before. All she had to say was *yes,* but she knew she couldn't. She had to offer to give Finder back.

"Tell Prince Shikry that I do love Finder, but I want him to have his dog. It's only fair, and I wouldn't feel right about using his gratitude to take Finder from him. After all, it was because of Finder that we were able to help him."

It was not easy to say these words, but she had said them, and she managed to keep smiling. Prince Abou watched her, then turned and translated what she had said to his nephew. Prince Shikry looked down at Finder. Then he looked at Jenny searchingly. Finally he spoke, Prince Abou translating.

"Prince Shikry says that you are very generous. He accepts your gift and hopes that someday you will visit him and the dog in his home."

The boy bowed as Jenny turned to him again. He was smiling, and she could tell that he was very happy. In spite of her own feelings, she couldn't help but be glad for him.

After that she was in a daze, and she was hardly aware of the gifts being given to Ron, Lauren, and the twins, and of the talk back and forth. There was one moment, however, that she remembered long afterward. Finder had wandered back to the boy, and suddenly Prince Shikry knelt next to him, signalling to Jenny with a quick gesture. Jenny hurried over, and fixing Finder with a glance, the boy spoke a command. Immediately Finder turned in the direction the boy was pointing and knelt with his front paws folded under. At a second command he touched his nose to the ground. Prince Abou, who was watching, explained that it was a trick Prince Shikry had taught the dog: to bow to Mecca. Jenny said that she wanted to learn the words, and when Prince Abou had translated this, Prince Shikry pronounced the words slowly, syllable by syllable, with Jenny mimicking the sounds until she had learned them. Then she put Finder through the trick to general applause.

Finally it was time for the boy and his uncle to go, and again there was handshaking all around. Mr. Martin said that if Prince Shikry should happen to be in New York in the future, he hoped that the boy would be able to visit them, and Prince Abou said that he was sure his nephew shared the hope. Then they climbed into the car with Finder in Shikry's lap and drove away. Jenny watched them go, then walked back into the house.

She was still dazed. One moment Finder had been hers, and the next he was gone forever. And it was her own doing. She had given him up of her own free will. She shook her head, staring down at his water dish. Then she picked it up and emptied it into the sink.

"Jenny."

Jenny turned. Her mother was standing in the doorway, watching her.

"What?"

"I want you to come with me. I have something to show you."

"What?"

"You'll see."

Taking Jenny's hand, she led her through the house and out the front door. Turning right, she led the way down the walk to the Rollins house, stopping as they reached the deck. Jenny looked around, puzzled.

"What is it?" she asked.

"Look under the chair."

Jenny looked where her mother was pointing and suddenly she saw it. It was a puppy: a soft, brown, cuddly bundle of half-grown dog that closely resembled Finder as he had looked when she had first seen him. Jenny stared in amazement. Abruptly the puppy gave a shrill bark and bounced up to her. Without thinking, she fell to her knees, and the puppy jumped back and barked again. Then Jenny reached out tentatively, and the puppy moved forward and licked her extended finger.

"It's yours, Jen," her mother said softly.

"I can keep it?" Jenny asked wonderingly.

"As long as you like. Your father and I have been house-hunting the last month, and we've bought a house on the mainland. We'll all be going over to see it tomorrow. This is your dog, your very own."

Jenny was silent for a long time, looking at the puppy, which looked back at her anxiously. Abruptly it cocked its head, ears slightly raised, as if it were waiting for a command. Jenny smiled in spite of herself. It wasn't Finder—there never would be another Finder—but it was a dog, and now it was hers. Slowly she reached out and picked the puppy up. It wiggled and squirmed in her arms, trying to stretch up to lick her chin.

"Do you think I'll ever see Prince Shikry again?" she asked softly, glancing up at her mother.

"It's hard to say. I was very proud of you today."

"I didn't want to give Finder up."

"I know, but as time goes by, I think you'll be able to look back on what you did today with a lot of satisfaction."

"What would you have done if I had kept Finder?" Jenny asked curiously. "Would you have given this puppy to someone else?"

"I never gave it a thought. I know my daughter."

Jenny smiled, scratching her new pet behind the ears. It still hurt, but she was already feeling better. Her mother was right. There was a real satisfaction in having done something difficult.

"Let's go back to the house," she said, getting to her feet. "I want to show the kids my new dog."